"Shelly, you'
Dr. Freeman
you to be disc
for your antibiotics. As soon as
this dose is in, you'll be released."

"Good." Shelly leaned back against the raised mattress of her gurney.

"There's only one condition," Jared added.

Her gut clenched. She should have known the doctor's capitulation had been too easy. "And what might that be?"

"That you allow me to sleep on your sofa overnight to keep an eye on you." Jared's normally somber gaze twinkled with amusement as her eyes widened in horror. "Don't worry. I'll promise to behave."

Behave? Maybe she didn't want Jared to behave...

AIR RESCUE—

**High-flying doctors—
high-altitude medical drama.**

Look out in April 2005 for the next dramatic
AIR RESCUE story—

THE DOCTOR'S RESCUE MISSION
by Marion Lennox

from Mills & Boon® Medical Romance™.

THE FLIGHT DOCTOR'S RESCUE

BY
LAURA IDING

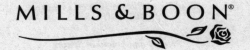

I'd like to dedicate this book to my critique partners, Denise and Kathy. Thanks for all the honest feedback and great Monday night sessions.

DID YOU PURCHASE THIS BOOK WITHOUT A COVER?

If you did, you should be aware it is **stolen property** as it was reported *unsold and destroyed* by a retailer. Neither the author nor the publisher has received any payment for this book.

All the characters in this book have no existence outside the imagination of the author, and have no relation whatsoever to anyone bearing the same name or names. They are not even distantly inspired by any individual known or unknown to the author, and all the incidents are pure invention.

All Rights Reserved including the right of reproduction in whole or in part in any form. This edition is published by arrangement with Harlequin Enterprises II B.V. The text of this publication or any part thereof may not be reproduced or transmitted in any form or by any means, electronic or mechanical, including photocopying, recording, storage in an information retrieval system, or otherwise, without the written permission of the publisher.

This book is sold subject to the condition that it shall not, by way of trade or otherwise, be lent, resold, hired out or otherwise circulated without the prior consent of the publisher in any form of binding or cover other than that in which it is published and without a similar condition including this condition being imposed on the subsequent purchaser.

MILLS & BOON and MILLS & BOON with the Rose Device are registered trademarks of the publisher.

First published in Great Britain 2005
Harlequin Mills & Boon Limited,
Eton House, 18-24 Paradise Road, Richmond, Surrey TW9 1SR

© Laura Iding 2005

ISBN 0 263 84290 8

Set in Times Roman 10½ on 12½ pt.
03-0205-41915

Printed and bound in Spain
by Litografía Rosés, S.A., Barcelona

CHAPTER ONE

FLIGHT Nurse Shelly Bennett slipped unnoticed from the debriefing area, seeking the relative peace and quiet of Lifeline's lounge. She sank onto the sofa and rubbed a hand over her bloodshot, gritty eyes. Nausea still churned in her stomach four days after learning about her five-year-old son's abnormal lab values. As a result of hearing the news, she'd stayed up late every night, surfing the net and devouring every bit of information she could find on pediatric renal failure.

She closed her eyes against an overwhelming surge of helplessness. *Please, God, he's just a little boy. Please keep Tyler healthy.*

''Good morning.''

Her eyes snapped open at the deep male greeting. A tall, blond-haired stranger with a square jaw and brilliant blue eyes, wearing a one-piece navy blue flight suit exactly like hers, stood a few feet from her. Shelly frowned and quickly stood. Who was this guy? Had she missed something these past few days in her concerned haze over Ty?

The stranger didn't seem to notice her confusion. ''Ah. I was hoping to find some fresh coffee here.''

''Good morning, Jared.'' Kate, one of her fellow flight nurses, instantly shot out of the debriefing room.

Fluffing her short blond curls, Kate eagerly stepped forward. "How was your move from Boston? Are you finally settled?"

"I still have things in boxes, but for the most part I'm moved in." He helped himself to a cup of coffee from a pot on the nearby counter, then turned toward Shelly, extending his free hand. "I don't believe we've met. Jared O'Connor, new Medical Director here at Lifeline Medical Air Transport."

Oh, yes, she remembered now. Shelly nodded and forced a smile as she took his hand in greeting. Despite her worry over her son, a tingle of awareness skipped down her spine as she shook hands with her new boss. Dr Jared O'Connor's hand radiated a gentle strength as it held hers and she found herself oddly reluctant to let go.

His distinct East Coast accent brought her back to Ty's father's family and the fact that Marc's last name had been O'Connor, too. She'd encountered a few O'Connors over the years, but the coincidence jolted her just the same.

Abruptly nervous, she cleared her throat. "Shelly Bennett, Flight Nurse. Pleased to meet you, Dr O'Connor. Welcome to Lifeline."

"I'm happy to be here. But, please, call me Jared." He eyed her over the rim of his cup. "Shelly. You're one of the pediatric specialty nurses, aren't you?"

She flushed at his intent perusal, wondering if somehow she'd betrayed her unexpected flash of awareness. "Yes."

"Good to hear. My background is pediatrics, too,

which explains why we've been paired to fly together.''

"Lucky duck," Kate muttered under her breath.

"Great." Shelly tried not to show her inner dismay. This couldn't have been a worse time for her long-ignored hormones to wake up over some man. There was only room for one male in her life: her son, Tyler. Lifeline was small enough to make avoiding Jared difficult but if they both worked peds, there was no hope of that at all. Being stuck in the sardine-like confines of the helicopter with Jared O'Connor was a complication she didn't need.

Was it possible he was related to Marc's family? Trying to control a flash of panic, she subtly searched his features for a sign of family resemblance. Thank heavens, she didn't find any. Marc had had brown hair, golden brown eyes and a lighthearted attitude toward life. Jared's blue eyes were solemn, his blond hair thick. He was taller than Marc and more than just physically attractive—there was an intensity about him that called to her on a basic level. Her unwelcome reaction was so foreign she took an automatic step back, nearly tripping over the sofa behind her.

Squaring her shoulders, she forced herself to think logically and not about Jared's almost imperceptible grab should she have fallen. There were hundreds of O'Connors in the Boston phone book. Marc's father was a lawyer, not a physician. Marc himself had been in law school before he died. Calmer now, she relaxed a bit, still aware of how Jared watched her. Their previous medical director, Dr Frank Holmes, had been

from Boston, too. No doubt, Jared O'Connor's presence here was as a result of his working with Dr
Holmes in the past, nothing more.

Now, if she could just ignore her ridiculous reaction to him, she'd be fine. Hopefully, Jared was happily married and completely unavailable. She allowed
herself to look in Jared's direction, boldly meeting his
intent gaze.

''So, can either of you give me some idea which
restaurants are good around here?'' His question included them both, but his gaze didn't leave Shelly's.
''I'm not big into cooking for myself.''

''Oh, is your wife moving later, then?'' Kate's
keen gaze belied her innocent question.

''I'm not married.'' His blunt tone didn't invite
questions.

Shelly's hopes plummeted and crashed to the floor
at her feet. So much for him being unavailable. If he
had been in a relationship, he obviously wasn't any-
more. She pasted a smile on her face and hoped her
dismay and attraction didn't show.

''Well, then, there's lots of great places to eat.
La Fluente's, if you like Mexican...'' Kate continued
enumerating various restaurants, announcing her interest in easing his solitude.

Jared's gaze finally unlatched from Shelly's and
swung toward Kate. Shelly let out a soundless sigh
of relief, grateful for her co-worker's outgoing nature.
Of course, Jared would be more interested in a cute,
willowy blonde than a round, curvy, rather plain bru-
nette like herself. She glanced at her watch and noted

there was twenty minutes until the start of their training session. Easing toward the door, Shelly figured she'd better head out to the hangar to make sure their pilot, Reese, had everything ready. She wasn't needed here.

Kate Lawrence held Jared in the palms of her very capable hands.

Jared frowned when Shelly slipped away, leaving him with the loquacious blonde. Thankfully, Kate's name was neatly printed in block letters above the gold wings mounted on the name tag secured to her flight suit or he might have forgotten it.

"Thanks for the information, Kate." He took another sip of his coffee and glanced toward the door Shelly had disappeared through. "I missed morning report but noticed there's a training class scheduled for today."

"Yes. Because we're affiliated with the medical school, we teach several emergency-trauma classes for the new residents coming on board. As flight nurses, we get first crack at them, but eventually we turn their very green hides over to you." Kate smiled and he was suddenly struck by how young she was. She was so full of life she reminded him painfully of his younger brother. Marc had been the same way, intent on living life to its fullest. At least, until the moment he'd driven his car at the estimated insane speed of eighty-five miles an hour into a concrete freeway divider.

Pushing aside the constant ache of guilt, Jared followed Kate outside. "Hope you don't mind if I watch." Immediately, his gaze sought out Shelly. There was something about the pediatric flight nurse that intrigued him. Maybe it was the air of fragility in her heart-shaped face. Or the sorrow darkening her pretty green eyes that made him wonder who or what had put those shadows there.

Kate reminded him of his brother, but Shelly was more like him. Her eyes told of deep anguish, heartache and loss.

Similar chords resonated in his heart.

Jared tried to listen to what Kate was rambling about, but it wasn't easy. His attention tended to wander toward Shelly, who was speaking quietly to Reese Jarvis, the pilot on duty today. Were the two of them close? With a frown, he stared at them intently. There was nothing in the way they stood next to each other to suggest it, and she didn't wear a wedding ring— not that the absence of a ring meant anything. Still, he couldn't imagine a woman as beautiful as Shelly not having a man in her life. If not Reese, then someone else.

Why did he care? He was a loner, always had been. More so since that horrible crash six years ago that had taken his brother's life.

His fault. Jared had learned to live with the knowledge that his argument with Marc had caused his brother's death. The gut-wrenching guilt wasn't fresh but still existed deep in his soul. There was nothing he could do to give Marc his life back, but he could dedicate his life to saving others. And to finding Marc's runaway fiancée and child.

But that wasn't the only reason for traveling halfway across the US. He'd worked with Frank Holmes, the former medical director of Lifeline, as a resident. When Frank's position had become available, he'd jumped at the chance to take it. Director positions of medical air transport operations didn't exactly open up on a regular basis.

His hope of finding Leigh Wilson was slim, but he wouldn't give up. Not like their useless private investigator had. Milwaukee wasn't as big as Boston, but trying to find Leigh Wilson here was too much like looking for a needle in a haystack. Restaurants were at least a place to start. Leigh had been working as a cocktail waitress at Stephan's, an elite club in Boston, when she'd met his brother. Six years was a long time, how did he know for sure Leigh had continued to work as a waitress? Yet that was the only lead he had. The thought of a single mom, struggling to make ends meet without the benefit of a college education, gnawed at him.

Jared's attention was snagged by a group of four residents, split equally male and female, entering the hangar. Kate and Shelly greeted them and quickly introduced themselves.

"Welcome to Lifeline." Shelly took the lead. "First, we'll go through some of the basics. Lifeline provides a transport service with two helicopters and one ground transport vehicle. We log over a thousand flights per year. You will each need to pass several classroom training sessions prior to being allowed to fly. Your first fifteen flights will be performed under the observation of another MD. After that, you're on your own.''

Distracted by the gentle curve of Shelly's neck as she bent closer to hear a question, he stopped listening. She was unconsciously graceful. His body stirred, responding to the picture she made. Confident in her position, yet seemingly vulnerable at the same time, her smile didn't quite reach her eyes. Dark brown hair waved gently around her shoulders. His fingers tingled with the need to touch, testing the strands to see if they were truly as soft as they looked. He averted his gaze.

What was he thinking? Shelly Bennett was off limits. There wasn't room in his life for a woman. Not unless that woman happened to be Leigh Wilson. And even then, all he really wanted was to meet her child.

His long-lost niece or nephew.

The call came in just as Shelly wrapped up her portion of the resident training session.

''Shelly, we're on.'' Jared waved her toward him.

''What's up?'' She asked, even as she grabbed her pager, carrying the same message.

''Eight-year-old girl with severe hypothermia. She's at Cedar Ridge Hospital, and they're requesting an immediate transfer to Children's Memorial.''

There was no time to be nervous about her first flight with her new boss. Shelly nodded and jogged toward the hangar.

Reese already had the chopper revved up and waiting. Jared grabbed his helmet and ducked inside. She
followed, then closed the light aluminum door behind
them. Once their helmets were connected to the intercom, they listened as Reese briefed them on the
weather conditions, then radioed the tower. The interior of the helicopter was tight but compact. Medical
supplies were mostly held in a large carry-on pack,
but some extra supplies lined the sides, looking messy
although everything had a place. They buckled themselves into the parallel twin seats, then listened as
Reese lifted off.

The ear-splitting drone of the engine, muffled by
the helmet she wore, had the strange effect of making
Shelly hyper-aware of Jared's presence beside her. He
seemed larger, with a broader chest, compared to the
other flight physicians she'd worked with. When he
shifted in his seat, his elbow bumped into hers. Shelly
tried to make herself smaller, hunching her shoulders
and clasping her hands in her lap, giving Jared plenty
of room.

Neither spoke, although their helmets contained
microphones and headsets for communication. They
listened as Reese interacted with the base regarding
his flight plan and verifying the location. Her gut
clenched as the chopper banked in a steep curve.
Though she'd been flying for two years, the sensation
never failed to give her a thrill. Adrenaline zipped
through her bloodstream, and she forced herself to
relax and focus on their mission.

Specializing in peds had been her choice long ago.

But now, with her son's illness hovering in the back of her mind, she couldn't help but wonder if she could maintain her objectivity. Sick kids were more difficult yet usually more rewarding to take care of. If she could keep her emotions in check. She shivered. Would the eight-year-old girl remain stable until they arrived?

The trip seemed to take forever, although it was really only twenty minutes' flight time. When they landed, Shelly was surprised when Jared helped pull the gurney out of the hatch. He clearly felt his role was to be an equal member of the team. She ditched her helmet and Jared followed her example before grabbing his side of the gurney. He ran alongside as they headed through the doorway and into the elevator that would take them down into the small community hospital's emergency department.

"Thanks for getting here so quickly." A harried female doctor greeted them from the young girl's bedside. "Annie Reed fell off her family's boat into Lake Michigan. Luckily, she was wearing a life vest, but she was in the water for a half-hour. Core temp is barely thirty-two degrees centigrade. We intubated her and put a warmer on. But her vitals aren't good."

Shelly swallowed hard as she quickly began to switch the connections from the hospital's monitors to their portable equipment. She listened as Jared discussed Annie's condition with the physician. Annie's heart rate was abnormally low, as was her blood pressure. The girl's parents were at the bedside, the poor mother sobbing as her husband held her tight. Shelly identified only too well with the mother's pain. It took all of Shelly's concentration to block a sharp wave of empathy and focus only on Annie.

The girl was small, barely thirty-three kilos. When Shelly slid an arm under Annie's bony shoulders, intent on moving her, Jared broke off his conversation with the ED physician to reach across and help her. His fingers brushed against hers as they seamlessly shifted Annie to the gurney.

There was no reason on earth for Shelly to be aware of the purely accidental and all too brief touch of Jared's hand on hers. Annoyed, she fastened the safety straps over her patient with a decisive click.

"Ready?" Jared glanced at her questioningly.

She nodded. "Do you have the transfer paperwork?"

"Yeah, it's all set. Let's go." He began to roll the gurney forward.

"Wait! We want to come with you." Annie's mother broke free from her husband, reaching out to clutch the frame and pull back on it, as if to hold her daughter there.

Jared paused, his gaze softening with regret. "I'm sorry, ma'am, but our policy prevents you from riding in the helicopter. You need to let us take care of Annie. I promise, you can see her as soon as you get to Children's Memorial."

Shelly watched as the woman's face crumpled in tears. She completely empathized with the woman's anguish. Her fingers tightened on the gurney as her stomach clenched. If the situation were reversed, there was no way on earth she'd let her son go alone without a fight.

Annie's father grasped his wife's shoulders and pulled her close. "Shh. It's OK. We'll drive down. Give us time to pull ourselves together. Annie needs us to be strong."

At least Annie's mother wasn't facing this on her own, Shelly thought as she tucked the warming blanket more closely around Annie's shoulders. As much as she was tempted to bend the rules by offering the woman a ride, she managed to hold her tongue.

In wordless agreement, she and Jared wheeled Annie through the ED and into the elevator leading to the helipad. Once they'd stowed Annie safely inside the chopper, she and Jared donned their helmets, then Jared gave the thumbs-up to Reese who quickly lifted off.

Jared bent over Annie's head from his seat, double-checking the various monitor readings, taking care not to disturb the warmer that covered her from neck to toe. Shelly worked from the bench seat along the side. His spicy aftershave penetrated the normal scent of fuel. Momentarily distracted, she frowned when Annie's blood pressure dropped further. Before Jared could say anything, she quickly double-checked the vasopressor medication and increased the dose.

She flushed when he gave her a quick smile and nod of approval. With an effort, she focused on her patient. Considering they were virtual strangers, their care of Annie was surprisingly in sync.

"Core temp up to thirty-two point three," she informed him through the headset. "I've switched to warmed IV fluids."

"Her heart rate is irregular. I'm double-checking the vent settings. Get the defib ready."

"It's ready." Shelly's own heart began to beat faster as she confirmed lead placement, then hit the charge button, just in case.

Jared's expression of deep concern, without any hint of arrogance, made her silently admit he was a very good physician. She stared at Annie's pale, yet perfectly formed, features. Her son's face held the same sweet innocence.

Once again, doubt nagged at the back of her mind. Could she continue to handle working with sick kids? Or would she constantly imagine her son's face transposed onto the features of every child she transported?

CHAPTER TWO

JARED was secretly amazed at how easy it was to work with Shelly. She anticipated what he wanted before he asked. Clearly, she was exceptionally bright or very experienced, although she didn't appear old enough for the latter.

"More PVCs," she informed him through the headset, even as she grabbed a syringe of Lidocaine and held it out to him for verification.

"Give a bolus of thirty-two milligrams," Jared ordered with a nod, before reaching for the radio controls that would bring him into contact with the ED physician waiting for them at Children's Memorial. He had a bad feeling little Annie wasn't out of the woods yet. "I'm requesting a hot unload."

Within five minutes, the helicopter hovered then landed with the grace of a dove. Jared barely noticed Reese's expertise, more intent on his patient's irregular heart rhythm. The hatch swung open, revealing a medical team from the ED waiting for them.

"Core temp still low at thirty-two point five," Shelly told him as they prepared to unload their patient.

Jared tucked the thermal blanket tighter around Annie as the medical team grasped the edges of the gurney, lifting it out of the chopper and springing the wheels so they could set it on the ground. He and Shelly hopped out after her. As he was still the physician in charge, he didn't take his gaze off the monitor.

"More PVCs. Increase the Lidocaine drip," he ordered.

Shelly adjusted the rate of the pump as she ran alongside the gurney and into the elevator that would carry them straight down to the ED. Jared couldn't relax, not until he'd handed over Annie's care to the ED physician.

The doors opened into the emergency department with a bang. The closest bed in the trauma bay was ready and waiting for them. Jared noticed that Shelly immediately grabbed the monitoring cables closest to her and began to switch Annie's equipment over. On the other side, an ED nurse helped do the same.

Jared provided Annie's history and condition as concisely as possible. When he'd completed his update, he asked, "Do you have a PICU bed open for her?"

"Yeah. I've already notified the peds ICU intensivist. He's on his way down." The ED physician accepting the handover of Annie's care nodded at them. "Thanks for getting her here so quickly. Her rhythm looks better now."

"Her temp is up another one-tenth of a degree," Shelly murmured.

Jared glanced at Shelly, but her attention was riveted on Annie's pale face, her expression grave. He couldn't help but wonder what was going through her mind. They'd managed to get their patient here without any major catastrophe in flight. Annie seemed to be doing better, but Shelly still looked as if she'd lost her best friend.

Why did he have this insatiable need to know intimate details about Shelly? Obsessing about his flying partner, his subordinate, if he were to get technical, wasn't smart. He resented the way Shelly so easily replaced his brother's fiancée in his mind. Finding Leigh was more important than satisfying his curiosity about Shelly's personal life.

He and Shelly stayed close at hand until they were sure their help was no longer needed. Once the pediatric ICU physician transported Annie to the PICU, their job was over. Watching them leave with Annie was difficult. Jared curled his fingers into fists. He'd made the decision to give up his pediatric surgical residency in favor of pediatric emergency medicine after his brother's death. He generally liked emergency medicine but times like this were difficult.

A glance at Shelly proved she appeared as forlorn as he felt.

''She'll be fine,'' he murmured, touching her arm gently. ''We'll check on her tomorrow.''

''I know. It's just that this is the hardest part of our job, handing over the care of our patients to others then simply walking away.''

Jared silently agreed.

Shelly turned from Jared and led the way back to the elevator that would take them up to the helipad. The heat from Jared's touch lingered on her arm long after his hand had fallen away. Why this sudden yearning for someone to lean on? Hadn't she been doing fine by herself these past six years? Yet the vision of Annie's father, holding his wife, stayed with her for a long time.

Reese was waiting for them outside the chopper, which was painted a brilliant blue with the words LIFELINE AIR TRANSPORT boldly printed in white along the side.

"All set?" Reese asked, an unspoken question in his eyes.

Shelly nodded. "Yeah. She's OK."

Government regulations about privacy prevented her from giving out detailed patient information but, considering Annie couldn't have gotten here without Reese's help, Shelly felt it was only fair for him to know the general outcome. Reese grinned at the news and gestured for them to jump back into the chopper.

She tried to ignore Jared as he climbed into the seat beside her, but her lungs were tight, as if she couldn't get enough air. Listening to the familiar sounds of Reese talking over the headset helped her regain her equilibrium. Reese was a great guy. If she needed someone to lean on, he would be a good candidate. Reese possessed a quiet strength, with no indication of being a player, out for a good time. Still, she'd never had the urge to cross the line of amiable friendship, not with Reese or anyone else.

No, after years of living in a deep-freeze, her nerve endings had come leaping to life in awareness over one man.

Jared O'Connor.

Tough beans, she told herself firmly. Get a grip. Even if he was interested, which he wasn't, she didn't have time for him. Ty needed stability. She'd given her unborn baby a promise a long time ago, Tyler would not grow up with a long line of "uncles" in his life. Every ounce of her free time was spent with her son. Truthfully, she wouldn't want it any other way.

Her unruly hormones would just have to get over it.

There weren't any other calls the rest of her shift, an unusually slow day when she preferred to be busy. At seven-fifteen that evening, Shelly drove over to her sitter's house to pick up Ty. Ellen was picking up toys in the playroom when she arrived.

"How are you, big guy?" She laughed when her son launched himself at her.

"Mommy!" His arms clamped firmly around her neck but she didn't mind. She closed her eyes and clutched him tight, burying her face in his hair, reveling in the sweet crayon scent of childhood innocence. Dear God, how she loved him. Tears pricked her eyelids as she thought about his upcoming medical tests. Please, let him be OK.

"Did you fly today?" All too soon, her son wriggled in her arms, indicating he wanted to get down. Reluctantly, she loosened her grasp and set him on his feet.

"Yep. I flew today," she confirmed. Even at this

young age, Ty seemed fascinated with her job. He claimed he could see her in the bright blue helicopter high in the sky and always waved at her.

"Cool. I'm gonna be the pilot one day."

"You bet," Ellen responded to his comment as she picked up her toddler daughter and walked with Shelly back into the kitchen. "You'll be a great pilot, Ty."

"Hi, Ellen. How was everything?" Shelly asked with a smile.

"Great." When Shelly raised her eyebrows questioningly, Ellen shrugged and hitched her baby daughter onto her hip for a better grip. "Well, the usual, then. Alex and Ty had fun fighting over their toys. The good news is that no blood was spilled today."

"A good day overall, then." Shelly thanked her lucky stars that she'd met Ellen when they'd both been in the hospital, giving birth to their respective sons, Alex and Ty. Shelly had been fretting over child care and Ellen had commented on how she was planning to quit her job to stay home, but wouldn't mind a little extra income from baby-sitting. Uncertain at first, Shelly had soon met Jeff, Ellen's husband, who had wholeheartedly agreed with the idea. For five years Ellen had faithfully watched Ty, and just within the past month the boys had begun attending all-day kindergarten together.

"OK, Ty. Let's go."

"See you tomorrow." Ellen waved as they left,

adjusting her daughter on her hip so little Emma could wave, too.

"You gotta work tomorrow?" Ty asked in dismay, wiggling as she buckled his seat belt in the back of her car.

"Last day this week." Shelly shut the door, then climbed into the driver's seat. Shelly considered herself lucky to work three twelve-hour shifts a week, leaving four full days home with her son. One week she worked day shifts, the following week night shifts. Her body didn't like the night rotations, but less time away from Ty was better for him, so she readily put up with the schedule. She eyed her son in the rear-view mirror. "And don't make that long face at me. On my days off, all you want to do is go to Alex's house to play."

"'Cause Alex is my best friend," Ty announced. "We have the same birthday."

Shelly's smile dimmed. A best friend sounded good, but she certainly wouldn't know from experience. In all honesty, she wasn't really that close to anyone. Ellen was wonderful, taking care of Ty during her twelve-hour shifts each week, but they didn't hang out together on her days off. She and Kate got along very well, but Kate was also friendly with everyone and maintained a very active singles social life, one that excluded Shelly.

She shrugged off her self-pitying thoughts. What was wrong with her? Ever since finding out about Ty's possible renal failure, she'd been nothing but a mope. She needed to snap out of it. Hadn't she been in worse situations before?

Those dark days after she'd run from Boston hadn't haunted her for a long time. Fighting severe morning sickness, trying to finish her degree and take her state boards for her RN license, while working full time to save money, had caused those seemingly endless days to blur together. Remembering them now had the effect of cheering her up. She and Ty had gone through tough times and had come out just fine. Nothing could get between them now. Especially not some stupid illness. Whatever came of Tyler's diagnostic tests, scheduled in less than two weeks, she'd deal with it.

For what was left of the evening, Shelly maintained her positive attitude. Thank heavens, Ellen was wonderful enough to feed Ty with the rest of her family so, without dinner to worry about, they spent a half-hour playing Ty's favorite board game, Chutes and Ladders. Afterward, Shelly gave her son a snack, then read him a bedtime story. When the story was over, Tyler knelt at the side of his bed to say his prayers.

"Dear God, please bless Mrs Ellen, Alex, Emma, my mom and my dad up in heaven. Amen."

Shelly smiled gently as her son bounced into his bed. "Good night, Ty." She pulled the covers up and tucked them beneath his little pointy chin. "Don't let the bedbugs bite."

He giggled, as he always did at the silly saying.

Later that night, once again, Shelly couldn't sleep. After twenty minutes of tossing and turning, she gave up. This time, though, she couldn't bring herself to go online to read any more depressing information about renal failure. Instead, she turned on her bedside lamp then pulled out her journal. At times like this, it was best to get her thoughts down on paper and out of her head, where they tended to whirl incessantly until she dealt with them.

Marc, I'm so worried about Ty. This parenting stuff is hard enough, without adding a serious illness to the mix. I don't think anyone else but another parent can understand how difficult this is. I've read all about pediatric renal disease these past few days and it's so scary. I can't imagine putting Ty through special diets, dialysis needles and other painful procedures. He's just a little boy, he doesn't deserve this!

Did you have trouble with bladder infections as a child? Did your parents? It's times like this that I really resent you leaving me alone. I want answers, no matter how unreasonable that sounds. What if he needs a kidney transplant? The thought of anything happening to our son makes me cry. See? I'm already dripping tears on this as I write.

I've accepted the fact that we were never meant to be, even though Ty's illness has made me wonder about you and your family. Still, I refuse to wallow in the past. Ty is my future. If you have a way to infuse more strength into me from up there, please do. I'm going to need every ounce and then some, to get through Ty's illness alone.

Shelly.

*   *   *

Jared immediately noticed the dark circles beneath Shelly's eyes when she came into the debriefing area the next morning. Granted, zero-seven-hundred was early but, after barely saying good morning to anyone, she helped herself to a cup of coffee and slid into a seat off to the side, away from the others.

He frowned. His instincts shouted that something was wrong. Late last night, he'd reviewed the notes Dr Holmes had left for him regarding the Lifeline employees. Shelly's information indicated her pediatric specialty and the fact she was single, although he wasn't sure why Holmes thought her marital status was important.

Had she had a fight with her boyfriend? Bad news of some sort? He wished he knew Shelly well enough to ask, but he didn't. Sipping his coffee, he listened to the report detailing the cases the Lifeline staff had responded to during the night. There had been two inter-hospital transfers and a crash scene response where luckily the injuries hadn't been too serious.

There was an immediate callout for an adult patient needing inter-hospital transfer, ICU to ICU. Kate and one of the more experienced residents jumped up as they were scheduled to fly. Jared couldn't help a small feeling of relief that he wasn't going to be stuck with Kate. She was nice enough, but a little overpowering. And he hadn't needed Holmes's notes to know she was single.

As soon as the debriefing was over, Shelly disappeared. Into the lounge? He remembered finding her there yesterday morning, her eyes closed and brackets of concern tugging at her mouth. So maybe whatever was bothering her wasn't a new thing. He waited a few minutes, then followed. Before he got through the doorway, someone called his name from behind.

"Jared?"

He swiveled round to the paramedic who stood there. "Yes?"

"Phone call for you. Says it's important."

"Thanks." Jared retraced his steps to the report room. His office was in the back and he gestured toward it. "I'll take it in there."

Through his open office door, the paramedic nodded and waited until Jared picked up the phone before hanging up. "Hello?"

"Jared." His mother's tearful voice flowed over the line. "Your father's heart is getting worse. The doctors say his heart is only pumping at thirty percent."

A lump of concrete hardened in his gut. Jared closed his eyes, rubbing hard against his forehead. He'd known his father had heart disease, the old man had already undergone one open-heart procedure. But apparently his father had taken a turn for the worse.

"Did they recommend any other tests?" Jared asked.

"No. They said there's nothing more they can do. He's not a candidate for more surgery." His mother broke down, sobbing. "Oh, Jared—what am I going to do?"

"Please, Mom, don't cry." Yet Jared couldn't really blame her. His throat tightened and a throbbing headache started behind his eyes, but he forced himself to speak calmly. "Dad might not be a candidate for surgery, but he isn't hopeless yet. Lots of people live with only thirty percent ejection fraction."

He could hear his mother struggling to get her tears under control. "I'm sorry. I'm so worried. I wish you could come home, Jared, at least for a few days. Please?"

Familiar guilt slammed into him with the force of a 747 jet. He swallowed hard. "I've only been here for a few days but I'll try to arrange some time off in a week or so. Tell Dad I'll call him later. I'll also give his doctor a call, too."

His mother quietly blew her nose on the other end of the line, seeming to gather herself together. "I understand. I know your work is important."

Jared sighed and rubbed his temple. "It's not just work, Mom. I told you I'm trying to find her."

He didn't have to explain who he was trying to find, his mother immediately knew. "Oh, Jared. Do you really think you can? Even after all these years?"

"I don't know. The PI Dad hired managed to discover that Leigh's family had lived here in Milwaukee, but then he hit a dead end. Too many Wilsons and none of them with a daughter named Leigh. But when Dad fired the PI three months ago, I figured it was my turn. He didn't care as much about finding Leigh Wilson as I do." Jared scowled, still ticked at the PI's handling of the case, or lack thereof. A little investigation into the guy had revealed he was cheerfully spending the monthly retainer but doing nothing on the investigation to earn the money.

His mother's voice brightened. "Well, then. You'll call us when you have some news?"

"I promise. Now, pull yourself together. Dad needs you." Jared listened as his mother calmed down then finally hung up.

Jared dropped his head into his hands, overwhelmed by a feeling of hopelessness. He knew his father's health wasn't good, but apparently things were even worse than he'd thought. Not a candidate for surgery really meant there wasn't anything else the doctors could do for him.

He needed to find Leigh Wilson and her child soon. The trail might be cold after all this time, but he refused to give up. Surely there was someone here who had known her or her family. His dad deserved to see his only grandchild in the short time he had left.

"Jared?" A familiar female voice interrupted his thoughts. A gentle hand dropped onto his shoulder, squeezing gently. "Are you OK?"

He lifted his head, surprised to see Shelly standing beside him, her face pulled into a frown of concern. Her small hand radiated warmth through the fabric of his flight suit and he reached up to cover it with his.

"I don't know." He surprised himself by admitting the truth. "I just got a call from home about my dad's heart failure. According to my mom, there isn't anything else they can do for him."

"I'm sorry." Shelly didn't pull away from his touch and his pulse quickened, taking the small victory as a good sign. "Maybe you should take a few days off, go home for a bit."

Jared almost laughed at her words, an echo of his mother's. The light pressure of her hand on his shoulder helped ground him. He brushed his thumb over the satiny smoothness of the back of her hand. "Thanks, but he isn't that bad, at least not yet."

"Maybe not, but this must be hard for you, especially being far from home."

Jared tilted his head to get a better look at her. "You sound as if you're speaking from experience."

Her expression clouded over and she subtly pulled her hand from beneath his, taking a step back. Regret swelled as he instantly missed the physical connection. "Possibly. I won't know for sure until the tests are back."

"Your parents?" Jared couldn't help prying for more information. At least this explained the apparently sleepless night she'd spent.

"No. My parents are dead." Her expression closed and Jared battled a sense of frustration. He wanted to help her, to protect her from worry. But clearly she wasn't going to let him.

"I'm sorry to hear that." Who were the important people in her life? he wondered. There must be someone. Someone undergoing tests of some sort. Why wouldn't she tell him?

"Long time ago." Shelly shrugged, then cleared her throat. "I came in to let you know I'm heading over to do a follow-up on Annie. I'll have my pager on if we should get a flight call."

Jared rose to his feet, then hesitated. She hadn't exactly suggested he go along. Besides, he couldn't waste any more time. His father's health wouldn't last for ever. He needed to find Leigh Wilson and fast. ''Go ahead. Let me know how Annie and her parents are doing.''

''OK.'' She gave him an odd look. Had she expected him to accompany her? Then in a flash the strange expression was gone. She gave him a brief smile, then turned and left his office. Against his will, his gaze followed her curvy figure, flatteringly displayed in her flight suit.

He tried to ignore the emptiness of his office after Shelly had left. What was it about her that drew him so strongly? He'd met plenty of beautiful women before but none had affected him like this. After making several phone calls, he had a list of restaurants and clubs to check regarding Leigh. But his mind kept drifting back to Shelly.

She was a toucher, a nurturer. He liked being the recipient of her caring a little too much. But the way she bore the weight of her troubles alone bothered him. If there was some important man in Shelly's life, he hoped the guy appreciated how lucky he was to have her.

The mere thought of someone else offering Shelly comfort, though, depressed him more than the possibility of never finding the missing Leigh.

CHAPTER THREE

JARED worked on reviewing Lifeline's financial statements until a callout came in. He read the display on the pager, then called down for more information.

"A semi-truck jackknifed into multiple motor vehicles on the interstate. At least one family with kids involved," the dispatcher told him.

"Flight conditions?" he asked.

"Clear skies so you're good to go. One Lifeline crew is already at the scene."

Jared hung up the phone then headed outside to the hangar.

Shelly was already there, once again talking to Reese. Even as he watched, Shelly gave the pilot's arm a quick squeeze, before glancing down as her pager went off. Jared frowned. So was there something between Shelly and the pilot after all?

"Ready?" He couldn't help the sharp bite to his tone.

Shelly glanced up in surprise. "Of course."

Reese took his cue and gave them the quick rundown of the location and flight plan. Within minutes, they were airborne.

Jared wanted to ask Shelly how Annie was doing, but forced himself to stay quiet. Reese was keeping in contact with the base and getting information on where they could land. Through the chopper's window, Jared could see swarms of paramedics and firefighters amidst the smoke rising from the crash scene. The first Lifeline helicopter was still there, too. For a moment, he was strongly reminded of the night his brother had died.

Shaking off the unwelcome memories, he followed Shelly out of the helicopter the moment Reese landed. They were instantly flagged down by one of the paramedics.

"There are three kids trapped in that green van over there," he directed them. "We're still trying to get them out."

"Any kids in the other wrecks?" Jared asked, unable to tear his gaze from the wreckage. There were crushed and mangled cars everywhere.

"No, thank God. But we do already have one dead victim, the driver of the first car the truck hit. The van was the second vehicle hit and the kids' parents are in bad shape."

As the guy spoke, Jared saw a badly bruised and battered man lying on a stretcher, being quickly wheeled into the first helicopter. Marc? He took a hesitant step forward, then abruptly pulled himself around.

No, not Marc. Marc was dead. Just like the driver of the car was dead. He shook his head to dislodge the painful memories. Why were they suddenly haunting him now? Because of his renewed vow to find Leigh? He blinked and realized Shelly had already dashed over to the van. There were kids inside the

crushed van that needed him. Shelly crouched beside
the firefighters who had already sawn off the door.
As he watched, she crawled inside the wreck.

"What are you doing?" Panic surged and he
rushed forward to grab her arm, preventing her from
going further.

She shot him an incredulous look over her shoulder. "Those kids are scared and crying. I'm the smallest one here, therefore the most logical to help get
them out."

He didn't like it, didn't like the potential danger.
But if the situation had been reversed, he'd have done
the same thing. From inside the van, he heard the
muffled sounds of crying. At least crying was a good
sign. Complete silence would have been much worse.
His resolve wavered.

"OK. I'll see what else we can do to help." Jared
let go of Shelly's arm. Her petite figure wiggled
through the door space and disappeared inside the
van. He turned to the firefighter still working on en-
larging the opening with the saw.

"Need another hand?" He waited until the guy
took another chunk of metal out of the van to offer
his help.

"Nah, I have it."

Helpless, Jared couldn't do much but watch. And
wait. He remembered the twisted metal wreck that
had been Marc's car after the accident. Had the re-
sponders to the scene worked like this to get him out?
Had they known that it had been too late, that Marc
had died on impact?

"There, that's a large enough opening, I think."

Jared realized the firefighter was talking to him. *Come on, man, focus,* he lectured himself. *Marc is gone. These kids need you to rub a few brain cells together and think.* He nodded at the firefighter, then climbed partially inside the van.

He blinked, waiting for his eyes to adjust to the dim interior. Just barely, he could see Shelly wedged between the seats, trying to free the kids. "Shelly? How are they?"

The crying had quieted and Jared didn't know if that was good news or bad. He hoped Shelly's presence had calmed the kids.

"Not bad. Luckily, they're all in car seats. I'm freeing up the smallest one now. Get ready, I'll hand her over, in the seat."

Jared didn't know how Shelly could move, much less wriggle around enough to free the smallest child, a little girl who looked to be about two. There was some blood on the girl's head where she was cut. Her lungs worked well enough, though. She bellowed louder as Shelly handed her over.

"Shh, it's OK. I have you." Jared held the car seat close as he backed outside then turned to set it on the gurney. Her crying meant he couldn't hear much when he tried to listen to her heart and lungs. After a quick neuro exam, he let out a soundless sigh of relief. The girl must have been very cushioned by the car seat because, other than the cut on her forehead, she appeared to be fine.

He turned to the firefighter. "Where are her parents?"

"Already on their way to the hospital." The firefighter nodded toward the first helicopter lifting off from the scene. "They were both unconscious and badly injured. Took the brunt of the crash."

Damn. He hoped they'd make it. Summoning a smile, he nodded. "OK. Someone needs to hang onto this cutie for me, she needs to stay in the car seat until we get her to the ED." Jared handed the toddler over to a paramedic. "Tape the cut on her head with butterfly tape."

"Jared?" Shelly's voice called him from deep inside the van.

"Yeah?" He crawled back through the opening. "What is it?"

"There are twin boys back here and one of them has a broken arm. They were belted on either side of the car seat. I'm worried about possible neck injuries. Grab a couple of C-collars and a long board."

"Got it." Jared shimmied back out and grabbed the pediatric-sized long board from under the gurney mattress, then set two small C-collars on top. The board would only fit so far into the crushed van. "Can you reach it?"

Shelly didn't answer, but Jared could see her forehead wrinkled in concentration as she unstrapped the child and fitted one C-collar in place. The boy, whom he estimated to be about four or five, didn't like the restriction and started to cry. Shelly talked to him soothingly and kept his spine in alignment as much as possible when sliding him onto the board. Jared reached in, helping to maneuver him.

"I have him." Jared tried to give the kid a reassuring smile. "Hey, there, big guy, I bet you're hurting, aren't you? Well, we're going to fix you right up. Here, now, hold very still so we can get you out of here." He eased the child down the board and then strapped him on. Backing out of the van, he pulled the long board out with the firefighter's help.

They set the boy on the gurney as the little girl was still being held by one of the paramedics, then removed the long board so they could use it for the second twin. Jared saw Shelly was right. The boy's left arm was broken. He was also covered in minor cuts and bruises. Internal bleeding? Possibly, but he really hoped not.

"What's your name?" Jared tried to distract the boy as he started an IV.

"K-Kevin." He answered the question between hiccuping sobs.

"What's your brother's name? And your sister's?" Jared kept up a steady stream of questions.

"Kyle is my b-brother. K-Karly's the baby." Once Jared had given the boy a small dose of pain medication through an IV, the boy settled down enough so Jared could place a splint on his arm. Kevin would need to be taken to Children's Memorial as soon as possible.

Shelly emerged with Kyle, and between them they discussed with Reese the possibility of transporting both kids at the same time.

"What about their sister?" Shelly asked. "We can't leave her here. The parents are already en route to the trauma center."

Jared signaled for the paramedic holding little Karly to come over.

Shelly's face betrayed her distress. "Reese, what if the paramedic sat up front with the boy's sister? Would that impact the chopper weight limit? She's just a peanut and the car seat isn't much more."

"How much do you weigh?" Reese asked the paramedic.

"One eighty-five."

Reese debated for a moment, then nodded his consent. "We can do it. Let's keep the kids together."

"Good." Jared and Shelly hefted the twin boys and their gurneys on board. "It'll be a tight fit, but a short ride."

With their helmets on, he and Shelly could only talk to the boys one at a time, but soon enough they were on the roof of Children's Memorial.

They hadn't called for a hot unload, but the news of their arrival with three kids had already reached the emergency department and there were staff waiting for them when they jumped from the helicopter.

"Let's get these kids inside." The ED resident took Kevin, the more seriously injured of the twins, under his wing.

"Have you notified Social Services?" Shelly asked.

Jared knew what she was getting at. With the kids' parents' condition so tenuous, they would need to find extended family to take care of the little ones, and soon.

"Yeah, they're on it."

Within an hour, they had the boys checked out, confirming that Kevin did have some internal bleeding that resulted in a quick trip to the OR. Of the three, the two-year-old girl was the least injured. When it was time to leave, Jared noticed that Shelly's gaze lingered on the kids as she reluctantly followed him out.

"Are you OK?" he asked as they rode the elevator back up to the roof.

"Yeah. Fine."

He didn't believe her. Maybe he wasn't the only one with ghosts haunting him. "Hey, you did a brave job back there, getting those kids out of the wreck." Jared couldn't help but admire her ability to connect with kids. Heck, maybe he shouldn't be envious about a possible relationship between Shelly and the pilot. She deserved to have a family of her own.

"No braver than anyone else," she contradicted. "Those firefighters are probably still out there. Sometimes we have the easier job, just getting the victims out and bringing them in. Those guys will be out there for hours."

"Maybe so, but we also have the responsibility of life-and-death decisions." Jared nodded at Reese.

"All set?" Reese asked. Once again, the pilot's gaze was on Shelly.

"Yeah. The three should be just fine, but it's the

parents I'm worried about. I can't stand the thought of those kids being orphaned.''

Jared rested his hand on her back. ''I'm sure they'll find other family members to take them in.''

Her gaze dropped and her frown deepened. ''But what if they don't have any other family?''

''They will.'' He spoke with confidence, not liking to see her so sad. ''Those kids would win anyone's heart.''

Shelly just stared at him for a minute, then grabbed her helmet and plunked it over her head, preventing any further conversation.

But Jared sensed her thoughts remained troubled as they silently headed for home.

Those kids would win anyone's heart. Jared's words chased each other around and around in her head. Despite everything, she couldn't help but compare the twins' situation with her son's.

If she were suddenly injured, who would take care of Tyler? Oh, sure, Ellen would step in to help out, as would Kate or even Reese, but long-term? Who would adopt him? How would anyone know who Ty's father was, to find family for him? She didn't have any siblings and hadn't told anyone the truth about her past.

The idea of Ty being left alone in the world haunted her during the rest of her shift. Maybe she needed to do something, like leave some sort of will requesting Marc's family be contacted if anything happened to her.

The idea didn't sit well, but it was better than doing

nothing or leaving the decision regarding Ty's care to complete strangers. She glanced at her watch for the third time in ten minutes. Still an hour to go before she was off duty. Jared must have noticed her antsy behavior because he crossed over to her.

"Hey, how about we get something to eat at the hospital café across the street?" he asked. "It's close enough that we can still respond if there's a call."

Shelly stared at him for a moment, flabbergasted by his invite. "Oh, thanks, but that's OK. I, uh, want to get out of here on time. I need to get home."

Jared frowned then glanced at his watch. "Do you want to leave early?"

She did, but that would mean asking the night shift peds nurse to cover for an hour. "No, I can wait until Kristin gets in."

"The paramedic and I can cover for you," Jared told her softly. "The minimum flight crew for peds is either a nurse or paramedic with an MD. Go ahead and go home. You look beat."

Hesitating, she inwardly debated. Jared was right about the minimum flight crew on pediatric transports, but she took her responsibilities seriously. Leaving Jared alone didn't seem right. But the need to see her son was strong. Finally she nodded.

"OK, thanks." She hurried to grab her stuff from her locker. Back in the lounge, Jared stood in the center of the room where she'd left him.

He caught her arm as she brushed past. "Shelly?"

She stopped, swinging around to face him. "What is it?"

His eyes were so close, so amazingly blue. Almost against her will, she moved a step closer. His hand cupping her arm was strong yet gentle.

''I— Nothing.'' His hand slid up her arm to her shoulder, then tucked a stray strand of hair behind her ear. ''If you need something, let me know. I can help.''

His featherlight touch caused her pulse to jump erratically. Her eyes widened in surprise when he took another step closer. She stared at his mouth. Suddenly, she realized how badly she wanted him to kiss her.

Shocked, she took a step back, breaking the intangible connection between them. ''I...don't need any help. But thanks for the offer.''

Shelly grabbed her stuff from her locker, then left. Once outside, she let out her pent-up breath in a rush. That had been close. What in heaven's name was wrong with her? Jared was her boss. She shouldn't be thinking about what it might be like to kiss him.

Disgusted with herself, she hopped into her car and headed toward home, stopping at a small gas station long enough to grab something to eat. Ellen routinely fed Ty early with her family so Shelly tucked the sandwich away for later.

She was an hour early picking up Ty, but Ellen didn't mind. Shelly took Tyler home and made an effort to spend some quality time with her son. Emma's birthday was coming up and she helped him painstakingly color a birthday card for her. After he'd finished, she made him take a bath before going to bed.

Shelly took a bite of her sandwich as she surfed the Internet, seeking an online will form. When she found one, she printed it out and painstakingly filled in the information. She'd need to have the document witnessed, but felt better after taking action to make sure Marc's family would be notified if anything happened to her. More than halfway though her dinner, she noticed the sandwich tasted unusually awful, so she tossed the rest out.

Still restless, she picked up her journal again. Normally, she didn't write to him every night, but there was nothing normal about Ty's situation. And a one-sided conversation was probably healthier than none.

Marc, I wrote out a will today. Do you have any idea how hard it was for me to put in writing the directive to place Ty in the hands of your family if something happens to me? I never thought of things like this in those early days, after I ran from your family. But today I was reminded how fragile life is. I can only pray I remain healthy for many years to come.

Your parents were awful that day I showed up to tell them I was pregnant with your child. Of course, it was also the day after you died. Your mother scared me, shrieking about you and offering to pay me half a million to leave my baby with her. Dear God, Marc, money. She actually offered me money to give up my child. What kind of woman is she? How on earth can I leave Ty in her hands if something happens to me? Yet, without any family of my own, what other choice do I have? I can't allow strangers to care for him.

It's a no-win situation either way. I shudder to think what living with your parents would do to him. I know how much you complained about how they pushed you to become an attorney when you didn't want to. I'm still amazed that you planned to drop out of school without telling them. Still, look at how many years you bent to their will. I won't have Ty molded into some image they've created for him.

Our son has dreams of his own. Tyler wants to be a pilot when he grows up. I'll do anything to help him realize his dreams.

Shelly.

She set aside her letter to Marc, but somehow, right before she fell asleep, Jared managed to sneak into her thoughts, leaving her imagining once again what his kiss would be like.

Fiery, stabbing stomach pains woke her in the early morning hours. Hugging herself around her waist, she stumbled to the bathroom in the nick of time, losing the entire contents of her stomach in one horrible heave.

Shaking, she slid to the floor.

Her muscles morphed into rubber bands, weak and

quivering. The cramping pain in her stomach hit again, and she hung over the commode, gagging as though her body was intent on getting rid of everything inside her. Sweaty, she sat on the bathroom floor, feeling both hot and cold at the same time. When she tried to stand, her legs wouldn't support her. Her stomach cramps continued. Pain knifed through her belly. Oh, hell, it hurt. What was wrong with her? Why did this hurt so bad?

The minutes merged into hours but she still couldn't find the strength to crawl from the bathroom floor. Worry pushed through the agony in her stomach. Something wasn't right. Something really, really wasn't right. She had to find the phone. Ty shouldn't see her like this. With a Herculean effort, she pushed herself up but then collapsed again.

"Mom? What's wrong?"

She used a fraction of her strength to inwardly curse when Ty found her. Shelly attempted to smile in a feeble hope of hiding the intense pain that was much worse than when she'd given birth. For his sake, she tried once again to get up, but couldn't command her arms and legs into co-operating. What was wrong with her? More than a flu bug, that's for sure. Maybe a ruptured appendix?

Ty's features blurred as she tried to focus on her son. She blinked. "I'm a little sick, honey. Bring me the phone. Please? Mommy will call for help."

As soon as Ty left, she lowered her head against the cool side of the toilet. She didn't have the strength of a flea. Rivulets of sweat rolled down her back.

Deep in her heart, she knew there was something seriously wrong with her. Had writing up her will, appointing Marc's family as legal guardians, been some sort of premonition? Was she going to die?

Ty brought her the phone and it took all her strength and concentration to dial Kate at Lifeline.

"Hello?" a deep voice answered.

There was a loud buzzing in her ears. She couldn't place the voice on the other end of the line. She forced herself to concentrate. "Kate? Can I talk to Kate?"

"Kate's out on a flight. Shelly? Is that you?"

Jared. She closed her eyes against another searing pain. He was the last person she wanted to talk to, but if Kate was out on a flight, she didn't have a choice. Who else was on duty? She didn't have a clue.

"Yes. It's me."

"You don't sound good. What's wrong?" The concern in Jared's tone made her sag with relief.

"I'm sick. I'm sorry, but I need someone to help…" She had barely pushed those last few words out of her throat when the phone slid from her limp fingers. The buzzing in her ears grew louder, drowning out Ty's concerned chatter and filling her head with a roar.

Until at last there was blessed silence.

CHAPTER FOUR

JARED hung up the phone, his instincts screaming that Shelly needed help. *Now.* He leaped to his feet, then paused. Cripes, where did she live? He swore under his breath as he wildly searched through his employee files for the information. There. He yanked her file and flipped it open. His eyes zeroed on her address. He was most familiar with the area around the hangar, and luckily she didn't live far away. Clutching her address in his hand, he rushed from his office.

Ivan Ames, one of their pediatric paramedics, glanced up in surprise when Jared dashed through the lounge. "Call Dr Simmons to cover for me. Shelly's in trouble." He didn't so much as glance back as he exited the building.

Jared figured fate was on his side when he found Shelly's house without difficulty. The small, cozy ranch-style home was exactly the sort of place he'd have expected Shelly to live.

He threw the car into "park" and turned off the engine mere seconds before jumping out and running up the driveway to the house. Lifting his fist, he pounded on the door.

"Shelly? Are you in there? Open up." Jared tried the door handle, but the door was locked. Was she too weak to answer? He pounded again then stepped back, surveying the house to estimate which window might be the easiest to break.

The door abruptly opened but there wasn't anyone there. His gaze dropped. A small boy with sandy brown hair and big brown eyes, about the same age as the twins they'd rescued the other day, stood in the doorway.

"My mom is sick. Are you the 911 she called?" The boy's lower lip quivered as if he were about to cry.

Mom? His gut clenched in shock; he didn't know Shelly had a son. Still, he didn't waste time pondering the startling news or wondering where the child's father might be. He dropped down so he was at eye level with the boy, then spoke reassuringly through the screen door. "Yeah, I know your mom is sick. I'm Jared, a friend of your mom's. She did call me for help. I'm a doctor. Will you let me in?"

The boy regarded him soberly for a long moment, then nodded and reached up, standing on tiptoe to unlock the screen door. Thank heavens, Jared thought as he opened the door. The boy was right to be wary of strangers—the last thing he wanted to do was to scare Shelly's son.

"Where's your mom?"

"In the bathroom." The boy stuck his fingers in his mouth as he ran through the small living room, pointing to the first door in the short hallway.

If he hadn't been looking, he might have stepped on her head. Dressed in an oversize sleepshirt, Shelly was lying facedown on the floor, as if she'd tried to crawl from the bathroom but hadn't had the strength.

Jared's breath lodged in his throat. With an effort, he shoved his personal feelings aside and surveyed her as a physician. He knelt beside her, feeling for a pulse. The thready beat was present, but faint. Gently he shook her. "Shelly? It's Jared. Can you hear me?"

She didn't so much as move a muscle. Conscious of little ears hovering beside him, Jared swallowed a harsh oath. Where was the phone? He needed to call 911. She needed help, fast.

"Is my mom OK?"

Jared paused in the act of picking up the phone from the floor near Shelly's outstretched hand. If he called the paramedics, loud sirens and bright flashing lights from the ambulance would no doubt frighten the daylights out of Shelly's son.

He took a deep breath and reassessed the scene. She was alive, breathing on her own with a pulse. No need to panic. "We're going to take your mom to the hospital, OK?"

The brown-haired boy nodded, but his eyes were wide and apprehensive. Jared wished he could say something to reassure him. He reached out and gently rolled Shelly over, then knelt to lift her in his arms.

She didn't weigh much, but the mechanics of getting her off the floor while trying to stand were difficult, and he needed to use the wall to brace her as support. In the living room, he laid her gently on the sofa then turned back to the boy.

"What's your name?"

"Ty." The boy watched him warily. He wore thin Superman pajamas but his feet were bare.

"OK, Ty. I'm going to carry your mom out to my car. Can you find your shoes and socks?"

The boy scampered off, as if worried Jared would leave without him. Jared quickly took a moment to examine Shelly's pupils, and let his breath out in relief when they both seemed equally reactive to light.

What in the world had happened to her? Was she sick? Did she have some disease like diabetes that he wasn't aware of? Damn, he should have taken the time to read her personnel file more closely.

"Ready!" The boy sounded almost cheerful.

"Let's go." Jared lifted Shelly from the sofa. "Open the doors for me, Ty."

Shelly's son was a trouper, helping in every way that he could. Jared laid Shelly's limp form along the back seat of his car. When he eased out from the back seat, he found Ty standing there, watching him. Luckily the autumn day was warm enough that he wouldn't need to waste time searching for Ty's coat.

"Here, you can sit up front with me." Jared gestured to the passenger seat.

"Uh-uh. I'm supposed to sit in the back."

Jared rubbed a hand across his eyes. As a peds specialist he knew the importance of kids riding in a secure car seat and away from the dangerous passenger airbags. Yet time was of the essence, so just this once they'd have to bypass the normal safety rules.

"Ty, we have to hurry. I promise to drive safely,

but we don't have time to find your seat. Just hop in, you'll be fine. The ride to the hospital is a short one.''

The boy eyed him uncertainly, but then crawled up into the passenger seat. Figuring any seat belt was better than none, Jared took several precious moments to buckle Ty in.

By the time they arrived at the hospital, Shelly was starting to moan. Thankful she was beginning to wake up, Jared pulled right up into the ambulance bay at Trinity Medical Center's Emergency Department.

''I need help here! Bring a gurney!''

Two nurses rushed outside, wheeling a hospital gurney between them, then helped him get her onto it.

''What happened?'' one of them asked.

''I don't know. Shelly Bennett is a nurse at Lifeline. She called for help, said she was sick. I think she'd been throwing up. When I found her she was unconscious but had a pulse and was breathing.'' Hating to feel helpless, Jared racked his brain for anything to add that might help. ''I can fill out the initial information, then get back over to Lifeline to read her file. Maybe I can find out more.''

''Knowing her past medical history would be nice,'' one of them observed dryly. ''We'll see if she has old records on file here. Call us if you find anything significant.'' They quickly whisked Shelly away.

He stared after her, wishing he could do more. A little hand snuck into his and Jared glanced down in surprise. For a brief moment, he'd completely forgotten Shelly's son. The kid looked so forlorn, he instinctively reached down and lifted the boy into his arms.

"Hey, there. Guess what? Those nice people are going to take care of your mom. How about if we hang out together for a while?"

Ty's lower lip trembled and he held himself stiff in Jared's arms. "I wanna see my mom."

Jared's heart squeezed in sympathy. Cripes, the poor kid didn't even know him. Who were the familiar people in his life? Where was his father? He had no idea. But there were more important matters to attend to. Like getting his hands on Shelly's file. "I know you do. I promise, you'll get to see her soon. First we have to take a little ride."

Big fat tears slid down Ty's cheeks. For a moment Ty reminded him of his younger brother Marc. Five years his junior, Marc had been about the same age when their dog had died. Ty's tear-streaked face looked achingly familiar. But, unlike Marc, he didn't wail or cry. Instead, he simply laid his head on Jared's shoulder, snaking his small sturdy arms until they were wrapped tightly around Jared's neck.

He held the boy close, smoothed a hand over his back, longing to reassure him. The irony of the situation wasn't lost on him. Amazing how Ty was about the same age as his missing niece or nephew. Jared shoved aside the longing. He couldn't worry about Leigh Wilson or her child right now. Ty needed him. But he was as helpless now as he'd been twenty-two years ago in comforting Marc after their losing their pet. Until he knew exactly what was wrong with Shelly, there wasn't much he could say or do. Except keep Shelly's son company.

He'd promised the boy he could see his mother. On the brief drive to the Lifeline hangar, Jared vowed that when they returned, he'd keep his promise. Shelly would be fine and Ty would get to see his mom.

Waiting was pure agony. How did these families stand it? There was something wrong with the way the medical system worked. Jared and Ty had been waiting for over an hour for word on Shelly's condition.

Nothing.

Jared thrust his fingers through his hair in exasperation. What in the world was taking them so long? Since he hadn't found any additional medical information in Shelly's personnel file, he deduced they were performing a wide barrage of tests on her to figure out what was wrong. Still, the basic lab test results should have been back by now.

"I'm hungry," Ty announced. For one so young, the boy had been pretty good about the lengthy time they'd been sitting. "And I hafta go to the bathroom."

Jared glanced at his watch for the fifth time in ten minutes, stifling a sigh. "Let me tell the nurses where we're going, so they can find us when your mom is ready for visitors."

Jared quickly found the triage nurse, watching from

the corner of his eye as Ty jumped from one foot to the other. Apparently, he wasn't kidding about needing to go. "We need to take a break. Here's my pager number—please page me as soon as you have some information."

"I will, Dr O'Connor." The nurse flashed him a distracted smile. "We should hear something soon."

"Not soon enough," he muttered. Spinning on his heel, he returned to Ty and reached for the boy's hand. "Let's go."

Who would have thought a trip to the men's room would take so long? Ty immediately crossed over to the urinal on the wall, asking about it. Hadn't the kid ever been in the men's room before? Inside the stall, Ty locked and unlocked the door several times. After using the facilities, he stretched up over the counter to wash his hands then played with the auto-dryer machine until Jared put a stop to it.

"Your hands are dry enough. I thought you were hungry?" Jared raised his voice to carry over the roar of the dryer.

"I am." Ty nodded enthusiastically, pulling out of Jared's grasp to shove his hands back under the heat.

"Let's go to the cafeteria, then." Jared held the door open, gesturing for Ty to leave. "They're probably still serving breakfast. What are you in the mood for?"

"Hotcakes and sausage." Ty finally abandoned the novelty of the men's room and skipped down the hall to the elevator. "Mom loves hotcakes and sausage."

Really? Jared hid a smile. What little he knew of

Shelly, he couldn't imagine sausage was her favorite, but he could see her cooking Ty's favorite meal for him as if it were. He'd bet she was a great mother. With a frown, he realized Ty was still wearing his pajamas. Guess he wouldn't be nearly as good a father—heck, he hadn't even dressed the kid. At least Ty didn't seem to mind wearing his pajamas to the cafeteria.

As Jared ate, he tried to think of a subtle way to broach the subject of Ty's absent father. His pager went off. He read the ED number in relief. Finally, some news.

"Stay here a minute, Ty. I'm going to use the phone over there." He indicated a hospital house phone mounted on the wall a few tables from where they were seated.

"OK." Ty shoved a huge bite of pancake into his mouth, syrup dribbling on his chin.

Jared strode across the room, lifted the phone and dialed the number. When the phone was picked up at the other end, he identified himself. "This is Dr O'Connor. Did someone page about Shelly Bennett?"

"Yes, this is Erica, the nurse taking care of Shelly. She's awake. Do you have her son, Tyler, with you?"

"He's eating breakfast right now. Shelly's awake? Thank God. What did her lab tests show?"

"So far, we've ruled out a hot appendix and gallstones. She was severely dehydrated, so we gave her a couple of liters of fluid. She's weak, and still extremely nauseated. We're still working her up to find the source of her pain."

Jared frowned and rubbed his jaw. He'd thought for sure she had appendicitis. "What was her glucose?"

"On the low side of normal. We found her old records and she's not diabetic. Anyway, will you bring her son? She's agitated, asking about him, and I think she'll relax when she sees he's all right."

"Of course. He's almost finished eating anyway." Jared glanced back at the table but Ty's small brown head wasn't anywhere in sight. The blood drained from his face and he quickly slammed down the phone. Where was Ty? Frantic, his gaze searched the nearby tables. Good grief, he'd only been away for three minutes. How could the boy have disappeared that fast?

"Ty?" Jared wove between the cafeteria tables and chairs. *"Tyler!"*

"What?" Ty's small head suddenly popped out from underneath the table. Jared's breath left his lungs in a whoosh. The boy was safe.

"Don't do that to me." Jared's hands were shaking as he reached out to pull the boy close. Cripes, he was flunking Fatherhood 101. He'd almost lost Shelly's son.

"Do what?" Puzzled, Tyler cocked his head and pulled back. "I dropped my fork, see?"

Belatedly, Jared noticed the fork clutched in the boy's hand. By dropping his fork, Tyler had nearly shocked Jared's heart straight into asystole. "I was scared when I couldn't see you—never mind. Are you almost finished? Your mom is ready for visitors."

Tyler's eyes widened and he eagerly abandoned his plate, the fork clattering to the table. "I'm all done."

"Me, too." Jared grinned. "Let's go see your mom."

Shelly shifted on the uncomfortable gurney mattress, blinking at the brightness of the overhead lights. Everything was fuzzy, confusing since the moment she'd awoken on the wrong side of a hospital bed. If her stomach didn't hurt so much, she'd chalk the whole thing up to a bad dream.

But the pain was real. So was the nausea. Through her lashes she could see an IV bag dripping into her arm. Who had brought her here? And, most importantly, where was her son? She'd asked the nurse where her son was, and she kept saying he'd be there soon. But how could that be? Had they left him home alone?

The thought of Ty had her struggling against the weakness, pulling herself upright on the gurney with an effort.

"Whoa, there, where do you think you're going?" The nurse—Shelly thought her name was Erica—ran to her side and placed a hand on her shoulder to prevent her from sitting up too far. "Just take it easy and lie down. You're not going anywhere yet."

"Let me out of here. I need to find my son. He's only five, do you understand that? I have to find him!" Shelly knew she sounded hysterical but couldn't help it. How had she gotten out of her house and over to the hospital? Had the paramedics left Ty there alone? Maybe he'd been sleeping in his bed and they'd missed him. Or he'd hidden from them in fear. Dear Lord, she had to find him. She shoved the nurse's arm out of her way. She'd crawl out of here on her belly if necessary.

"Shh, I told you, your son will be here soon. He's with Dr O'Connor. They're on their way from the cafeteria now."

Dr O'Connor? Exhausted by her efforts, Shelly dropped back on the gurney and closed her eyes. Why was Ty with the doctor? Was Dr O'Connor performing Ty's kidney tests already? Had she brought him here, then collapsed?

"Shelly?"

Dazed, she squinted against the lights. A familiar blond-haired man stood at her bedside. The name finally sank into her shriveled brain. Dr O'Connor was Jared. Slowly, the events of the early morning came back to her. She'd called Lifeline for help. Jared had answered.

Jared had her son.

"Ty." Shelly focused her gaze on her son holding Jared's hand, standing beside him. Her throat swelled with relief. He was safe. Thank God, he was safe. "Are you all right?"

Ty nodded and Jared urged him further into the room. Ty grabbed the side rail, apparently willing to climb aboard, until Jared intercepted him.

"Hang on, I'll pull this down for you."

Jared lowered the railing. Shelly reached over and wrapped her arm around her son, lowering her head until she could lay her cheek against his silky fine hair.

Ty was fine. Still wearing his pajamas, sticky with a substance that smelt an awful lot like maple syrup, but otherwise fine. Better than fine. "I'm sorry, Ty. I didn't mean to get sick."

"Are you coming home now?" Ty asked.

"I don't think she's ready to come home just yet," Jared interjected.

"Yes, I'm coming home soon. I only need to rest." Shelly overrode Jared's objections, let go of Ty and relaxed back against the gurney mattress, sucking in a swift breath when her stomach cramped again. The doctor had reassured her that her appendix was fine. But, darn, her stomach hurt. If this was just a bad case of flu, she'd go home for sure. She needed a bathroom and no way was she using that bedpan, no matter how the nurse tried to sway her.

"Erica? I think Shelly needs help," Jared called out to the main arena.

The nurse came scurrying back. "What can I get you?"

"You can get me out of here. I need to go home. Where's the doctor?" Shelly wasn't in the mood to be poked and prodded. Why didn't they just let her lie in peace?

"Relax, I do have some good news. We found the source of your problem. Seems you have food poisoning in the form of an intestinal staph infection."

"Staph? From what?" Shelly wrinkled her forehead in puzzlement then her brow cleared as she

thought back to what she'd eaten after Ty had gone
to bed. "The sandwich."

Erica leaned closer. "Sandwich?"

"Yeah, my dinner last night. Tasted awful. I
dumped it, but not until I'd eaten more than half of
it." Shelly felt like a fool. Ending up in the emergency department of Trinity Medical Center just because of a lousy smoked turkey and mayo sandwich.
How humiliating.

"Ah, that's probably it." Erica smiled. "Well, at
least that's one mystery solved. We're starting you on
IV antibiotics."

"Good. Give me the first dose, then I'm outta
here." She knew she was being stubbornly persistent,
but didn't care.

"Not without twenty-four hours' worth of IV antibiotics." Erica's smile was strained. Shelly knew
she was a far from co-operative patient, but she
steeled her resolve. Ty needed her at home.

"I'll go home with my IV. I'm a nurse. I'm sure I
can hang a few antibiotics myself."

Erica threw up her hands. "Argue with the doctor,
OK? Leave me out of it."

When Dr Freeman walked in a few moments later,
he raised a hand as Shelly opened her mouth. "Hold
on, before you start nagging at me, I want to ask Dr
O'Connor a few questions."

Shelly snapped her mouth shut then narrowed her
gaze suspiciously. "Why? He doesn't have anything
to do with my care."

Jared's jaw tightened, but Shelly chose to ignore it.

So maybe she wouldn't be here without Jared's help, but that didn't give this Dr Freeman any right to discuss her care with him. But before she could blink, the two men left her alone with her son.

"We had hotcakes and sausage for breakfast," Ty chattered, seemingly not put off in the least with her being in the emergency department. "You should see how much food is in that cafeteria, Mom. There's loads and loads of stuff to pick from. Like, you can take anything you want. Can we stay here for lunch, too?"

Shelly flashed Ty a tired smile. "I don't know, we'll see. I'm glad you enjoyed your breakfast. It was nice of Dr O'Connor to take you."

"Is he your boyfriend?" Ty asked at the exact moment the two physicians returned to her room.

Mortification burned her cheeks. Good grief, where had Ty gotten such a wild idea? And she didn't even want to know what thoughts lurked behind Jared's eyes. He raised a brow in her direction but she was grateful he didn't pick up on Ty's innocent question.

"Shelly, you'll be glad to know Dr Freeman is willing to allow you to be discharged, with an IV for your antibiotics. As soon as this dose is in, you'll be released."

"Good." Shelly leaned back against the raised mattress of her gurney. "See, Ty? We'll be home before lunch."

"There's only one condition," Jared added.

Her gut clenched. She should have known the ED

doctor's capitulation had been too easy. "And what might that be?"

"That you allow me to sleep on your sofa overnight to keep an eye on you." Jared's normally somber gaze twinkled with amusement as her eyes widened in horror. "Don't worry, I'll promise to behave."

CHAPTER FIVE

BEHAVE? Maybe she didn't want Jared to behave. Maybe the only way she wanted Jared to come home with her was when Ty could stay overnight at a friend's house and she'd spent the day at an expensive salon, buffed and polished from head to toe. She flushed at her wayward thoughts, then dropped her gaze and bit back a groan. No way. What was she thinking? Jared was a complication. One big, testosterone-laden complication she didn't need. She didn't want him underfoot, behaving or otherwise.

Hoping he would assume her red cheeks were due to a fever, Shelly forced herself to face him. It was difficult to make a stand lying supine on a hospital gurney, but she gave it her best shot. ''I'm perfectly capable of taking care of myself. I'm not an invalid.''

''No one said you were.'' Jared's voice was calm. Reasonable. But she was so not in the mood to be rational.

Giving up on Jared, she shifted her attention to Dr Freeman. The older doctor stood with his arms crossed over his chest and a bland, almost bored expression on his face.

''Dr Freeman, I need to go home. Surely you can understand my dilemma. My son can't stay alone and I don't have family to watch over him.''

"Not even Ty's father?" Jared interjected.

She sent Jared a narrow look, wordlessly telling him to back off. "No." She shifted back toward Dr Freeman. "I don't understand why this is such a big deal. What could possibly happen to me that would need Dr O'Connor's attention?"

"Let's see, maybe you've heard of septic shock?" His condescending tone raked like fingernails down a chalkboard against her nerves. "Your choices are either to spend the night here in the hospital, while your son stays with Dr O'Connor, or go home under Dr O'Connor's care. This infection isn't anything to mess around with. If the antibiotics don't work, the infection could get worse. You need to rest, which will be difficult enough with a five-year-old around. Either way, the choice is yours."

Right. Some choice. She momentarily closed her eyes. Could this day get any worse? Grimacing, she quickly realized she was being totally selfish. Yes, things could be far worse. Ty could be the one stuck in a hospital bed, seriously ill with irreversible renal disease. She could be holding a crying boy in her arms as they stuck dialysis needles in him. She would gladly be sick if it meant he could be healthy. Abruptly, she lifted her chin, accepting her fate. "You're right. I'm lucky. I'll go home with Jared."

"Good. I'll see about getting your prescriptions filled in the pharmacy here." Dr Freeman grinned, although the thinning of his lips was more like a smirk, as if he enjoyed the role of master puppeteer, manipulating people's lives to his will.

"And I'll see if I can snag an IV pole for Shelly to use at home," Jared added cheerfully.

Shelly scowled at both of them. Twenty-four hours. Thanks to Dr Freeman's infinite wisdom, Jared would live in her small house for twenty-four hours. How bad could it be? Surely she could put up with anything for that long?

The moment the three of them entered her home, the magnitude of the situation hit hard. Shelly's spirits sank. Her house only had two bedrooms and while it was both affordable on her income and perfect for her and Ty, the interior shrank dramatically with Jared standing in her living room. The sofa pulled out to a sleeper, but she knew from experience it would take up the entire living space. They wouldn't be able to move without tripping over each other.

Resentment flared. She was so tired. The abdominal cramping returned, forcing her to gauge the distance to the bathroom. The IV fluids had helped, but every muscle in her body felt as if she'd been tossed in the washing machine with the dial stuck in the spin cycle. She didn't want to deal with Jared. Not when she could barely stand without hanging onto the wall for support.

"Come on, bedtime for you." Normally, Jared's no-nonsense tone would have made the hairs on the back of her neck stand up straight. Right now, she didn't have the energy to care, much less to fight.

"Mom's room is over here." Ty was absolutely no

help, skipping down the short hall and earnestly opening the door of her bedroom.

She scowled, wanting nothing more than to fall
face first into her bed and stay there for several hours.
But what did Jared know about five-year-old boys?
Nothing that wasn't in his *Merkt Manual of Pediatric
Diseases,* she'd bet.

"I'll rest soon." She forced a smile, hoping it
wasn't a grimace. "First I have to call the school, let
them know why Ty wasn't there today."

"I can call." Jared frowned at her. "Remember,
you need to rest."

"But Ty will need to have lunch soon and…" She
lost her train of thought. For the life of her, she
couldn't think of another reason to stay upright, although there had to be one, didn't there?

"Shelly." Jared leveled her a stern look. "Ty and
I will be fine. Better, in fact, if we don't have to worry
about you. I need to get the IV pole from the car set
up in your room before your next dose of antibiotic
is due. We don't have all day."

Her vision blurred, her eyes nearly crossed with
exhaustion. Had she been up half the night or did it
just seem like it? Finally, she nodded. "You win. Ty
will show you where the school phone number is and
there's food in the fridge." She frowned and tried to
remember the last time she'd visited the grocery store.
"I think. But maybe not."

"Bed. Now." Jared walked toward her and she instinctively knew he'd carry her if necessary. Her
fogged mind played tricks on her because she seemed

to know exactly how it would feel to be held by Jared, his strong arms wrapping strongly yet protectively around her.

The idea made her frown and she moved forward, ducking out of Jared's reach, making her way down the short hall under her own feeble strength. "I'm going. Just take care of Ty." She couldn't completely erase the wistful note in her tone.

Jared, thankfully, didn't follow her all the way to her room. But when she glanced back at him, she noticed he was watching her intently, a puzzled expression on his face. He wasn't a parent so he couldn't possibly understand how it felt to hand the care of your son over to someone else.

"I will. I promise, he'll be fine."

Despite her fatigue and cramping discomfort, Shelly nodded and entered her room. She changed, then crawled into bed. Jared brought the IV pole in, set it up, then hung the IV bag on the hook. She wasn't due for another dose of antibiotic yet and he quickly left so she could rest. But even when surrounded by the comforts of her own home, she couldn't lose herself in blessed sleep.

She heard the deep rumble of Jared's masculine voice followed by the delighted peel of Ty's laughter and wondered what Jared had said that was so funny. Ty was, no doubt, thoroughly enjoying the novelty of masculine attention. For a moment, uncertainty gnawed at her. Had she made the right choice all those years ago? Could she have tried to convince Marc's family to see reason?

Shelly squashed useless regrets. No, she knew she'd made the only decision she could have at the time. Single, alone and pretty much penniless, she couldn't have taken on Marc's wealthy parents and won. Not without a lot of luck. The risk of losing her child for good had been too steep a price to bet on luck.

Ty was happy. She'd provided a good home for him over the years. She didn't know why God meant for her to raise Ty alone, but she was determined to make the most of the path set before her.

Just before she drifted off to sleep, she silently acknowledged that she'd given Ty everything he possibly needed.

Except a father.

Jared grinned as Ty performed another in a row of somersaults that propelled him across the length of the backyard. The kid possessed a bottomless energy every adult coveted. After displaying his gymnastic expertise, Ty showed off his sturdy swing-set by climbing up to the very top.

"See? I told you I could," Ty gloated.

Jared winced, imagining his feeble explanation when Ty ended up in the emergency department with a cracked skull. He'd taken care of enough kids to know accidents happened, but they could also be prevented. He gestured for Ty to come down. "I see. Now come on down. Please."

As the afternoon wore on, Jared slowly realized Ty bore an uncanny resemblance to his brother Marc.

The boy's brown eyes and brown hair were similar enough to those of dozens of other kids but the little things, like the way his eyes crinkled at the corners and the hint of a dimple that flashed in his right cheek when he smiled, took him back several years. He imagined Marc had looked at him the same way Ty did, tilting his head to the side when listening to something Jared was saying.

Absently, Jared rubbed the nagging ache in the center of his chest. He was becoming obsessed with his brother. Memories of Marc had taken up residence in his head, telegraphing intermittent waves of guilt. Even now, he knew he should be searching for Leigh Wilson instead of playing baby-sitter to Shelly's son.

Jared sighed. Maybe he was kidding himself in thinking he could succeed where the private investigator had failed. He'd already logged several hours on the Internet on various search engines to no avail. Today he'd planned to head down to the Milwaukee County Courthouse to search all Wilsons living here during the time Leigh had been born. He'd hoped to start interviewing them one by one to see if he could find a relative of hers. There had to be an aunt or uncle, if not her actual parents somewhere.

''Mr Jared? I'm hungry. What's for supper?''

Good question. Jared glanced at his watch, noting with surprise that the time was close to six. It had been a few hours since he'd checked on Shelly. Ty had polished off an afternoon snack then, too, but obviously the kid needed to eat often to keep up with his speedy, bird-like metabolism.

"Let me check on your mom, she's due for her medicine, then I'll order pizza." Pizza was safe, wasn't it? From what he'd observed, every kid in the world loved pizza.

Ty's face clouded and he shook his head. "I don't like pizza. Besides, my mom says we shouldn't eat pizza 'cause it has too much salt in it."

Make that every kid in the world except Ty, Jared silently amended with a wry smile. Jared believed in eating healthily, too, but to ask a kid Ty's age to worry about eating too much salt was pushing the health notion a little too far. Unless there was some physiological reason why Shelly watched his salt intake? Pausing in mid-stride, Jared remembered the vague words she'd spoken that day in his office when he'd noticed her empathy in knowing how it felt to have someone you loved sick. She'd responded something about not knowing for sure until they ran some tests. He hadn't known about Ty at the time but now he wondered, was Ty the one who needed tests? Could there be something wrong with her son?

"I don't really like pizza, either," he quickly confessed. "How about a bucket of chicken instead?" There might be salt in the batter but he was pretty sure the local deli offered a heart-healthy version.

"Yum." Ty patted his stomach as Jared followed him inside the house.

Jared phoned the deli and placed the order, then walked down the hall toward Shelly's room. Although he tried to remind himself he was a doctor and she was practically his patient, he couldn't help but feel like a voyeur as he opened the door to her bedroom and crossed the threshold.

She was sleeping. For a long moment he stood in the dim room and stared at her. Despite having been so ill, she was really lovely. Her features were relaxed yet he clearly remembered the stubborn tilt to her chin when she was awake. Why did she resent needing his help? Or anyone's help, for that matter? She wasn't Wonderwoman, although the thought of the way she'd fought back while lying on a hospital gurney made him frown. Maybe he should check under her bed for a golden lasso. If anyone would have one, he imagined Shelly would.

His gaze followed the graceful curve of her jaw, the slender slope of her throat, then dropped lower still to her breasts, snug against the fabric of her sleepshirt.

Stop it! He tore his gaze away, inwardly wincing at his body's crass response. Shelly hadn't invited him here for a grown-up sleepover, no matter how certain parts of him wished otherwise. No, he'd bullied his way into her home, thanks to Dr Freeman's help. As a professional, gawking was strictly forbidden. Especially when the gawkee was asleep in her own bed and completely unaware of his presence as the gawker.

Jared didn't want to wake her, but she needed her antibiotic dose. Mini-bag in hand, he tiptoed across her room and quietly connected the tubing. He back-filled the medication bag, then frowned down at her, trying to remember which arm the IV was in.

A nurse would probably remember something like that, he thought with an inward grimace. Afraid of waking her, he leaned forward and eased her right arm out from under the blanket. Her skin was silky soft, and he had to fight the urge to linger as he realized the IV was, of course, in her left arm.

She shifted and murmured something as he turned his attention to connecting the IV, then opened the clamp, allowing the medication to slowly infuse. He tucked her arm back beneath the blanket, then backed out of her room before silently shutting the door behind him. After this dose, he'd cap her IV so it wouldn't clot, then Shelly wouldn't need another dose of her antibiotic until midnight. There would be no reason to go near her room until then.

Unless, of course, she asked him to come in. Which wasn't going to happen in his lifetime. Better for him to remember that fact. Not. Going. To. Happen.

Dinner went well and Jared was feeling pretty good about his temporary role as parent until Ty began to pelt him with questions.

"How come you don't have a little boy of your own?"

"Because I haven't found a woman I want to have a little boy with." He tossed the remains of their chicken in the trash.

"How come you haven't found a woman yet?"

Jared's lips twitched as he fought a grin. Ty was really something. "I don't know. Maybe women just don't like me."

"Hmm." Ty scrunched his face in concentration.

"You gotta talk nice to women if you want them to like you. No bad words or anything." Ty paused for a few seconds, then added, "Alex's dad brings his mom flowers. Maybe you should try that?"

"Good idea. I'll remember that one." Jared nodded sagely. "Now, tell me, what time are you supposed to go to bed on a school night?"

"Eight o'clock, although my mom always lets me stay up for special occasions."

"Oh, and I bet you think me being here with you is a special occasion, huh?" Jared knew when he was being hosed by a pro.

Ty's head bobbed enthusiastically. "Yep. Can we play a game?"

"Only if you agree to go to bed at your normal time of eight o'clock."

"Aw, do I hafta?"

"I'm afraid so. I'm sure your mother would agree if she were awake." Jared hoped Ty wouldn't put him to the test of waking her up but he wasn't adverse to blackmail if needed. He was pretty exhausted himself. Chasing Ty around had proved to be harder than he'd imagined. He'd have to give parents of small children more credit—heaven knew, they deserved it.

The boy's hopeful expression fell. "I guess."

Jared pulled out the sofa sleeper so they could play the board game on the mattress. Ty jumped on the bed until Jared grabbed him.

"Whoa, there. This isn't a trampoline."

"We can make it a trampoline!" Ty yanked himself out of Jared's grasp and proceeded to jump harder and higher.

With a groan, Jared tilted his head back, stared at the ceiling and wished the hands on the clock would move a little faster. Wasn't it eight o'clock yet? Why had he been stupid enough to mention a trampoline?

He began to explain why they couldn't possibly make his sofa sleeper into a trampoline but when Ty continued to argue why they should, he gave up. "Enough. No trampoline, end of discussion. Either we play this game or you go straight to bed." He felt a tad guilty laying down the law, but Tyler didn't hold a grudge for long. When Jared glanced at the clock again, he remembered how long Ty had spent in the men's room at the hospital and decided he should start getting the boy ready for bed a half-hour early.

Sure enough, Ty couldn't find his favorite pajamas so they spent a good ten minutes looking in every dresser drawer because Ty decided he couldn't sleep in any other. Ty finally found them deep inside his play-fort that masqueraded as his closet. After the toothbrush ritual and the complaints of being hungry and thirsty, the boy finally climbed into his bed.

"Good night, Ty."

"'Night." Ty's jaw stretched into a long yawn, then his eyes popped open. "I almost forgot my prayers!"

Jared hid a groan. He almost asked Ty to forget about it, then figured neither Shelly, nor God, would appreciate a brush-off. "You better say them, then."

Ty folded his hands under his chin and closed his

eyes. "Dear God, please bless Mrs Ellen, Alex, Emma, my mom and my daddy who is already up in heaven. Oh, and I almost forgot. Please, bless Mr Jared, too. Amen."

Speechless, Jared stared at Ty. Not only because he didn't think he'd ever been mentioned in anyone's prayers before but because of what Ty had said. His daddy was already up in heaven? Somehow he'd gotten the impression from Shelly that Ty's father was still around somewhere. When had Ty's father died?

He had to know. Crossing to Ty's bed, he sat down on the edge of the mattress. "Thanks for including me in your prayers."

"You're welcome." The boy yawned again.

He felt like slime, pumping Ty for information. But he had to know the rest. "I'm sorry your dad died. I bet you really miss him."

"Yeah." Ty nodded earnestly.

Jared's throat closed and he swallowed hard. "How long ago did your dad die? A few months ago?"

"No. My mom says he loved me a lot, but he died before I was borned."

Jared propped his arms behind his head, shifting on the hard mattress of the sofa bed. His thoughts wouldn't stop whirling in his head. Shelly's son was the same age as Marc's child. Both Ty's father and Marc had died before their sons had been born. The similarities between Ty's situation and Marc's long-lost child wouldn't leave him alone.

Shelly's last name was Bennett. Marc's fiancée's

name was Leigh Wilson. Shelly was a specially trained flight nurse, Leigh had been a cocktail waitress in a nightclub. He couldn't imagine they were the same person, but then he'd remember how much Ty reminded him of Marc and the doubts would return.

Of course, the truth would be easy enough to prove one way or the other. All he needed was a background check on Shelly. Was Bennett her maiden name or her married one? Heck, there was probably already a background check in her Lifeline file. As the medical director, it was his responsibility to know about his employees, right?

Wrong. He scowled at the ceiling of Shelly's living room. He knew darn well Shelly's personal past was none of his business. Unless she'd committed some sort of crime, which he was certain she hadn't. Unless she really was Leigh Wilson, which was so unlikely he couldn't believe he was even entertaining the harebrained notion.

He needed his head examined. From the moment he'd met Shelly his body had responded to her as a woman. She'd ripped his concentration to shreds, taking over his every waking thought until he had to force himself to focus on the real reason for being here—to find Leigh and her child. Easy enough to understand why he'd suddenly jumped to the easy answer, combining the two women messing up his head into one.

The creak of a floorboard caught his attention. Holding perfectly still, he strained to listen. Had Ty climbed out of bed? Was he going to his mother? Jared waited, trying to get a clue to the source of the noise.

Was that water running in the bathroom? Had Ty gotten up to go to the bathroom or was Shelly in there?

He hesitated, not sure he wanted to interrupt Shelly in the bathroom. The water stopped, and he thought he heard the door open. Then nothing. Everything was quiet. Shelly must have found her way back to bed.

Jared sighed and relaxed against the cushions he was using for a pillow. Now that he was awake, he wasn't sure he'd be able to fall back to sleep. Especially since he could all too easily imagine following Shelly into her room and into her bed.

A slight sound, like the rustle of clothing, had him opening his eyes, peering through the darkness. Then he heard a thud and a muffled groan moments before something womanly soft, yet round in all the right places, fell directly on top of him.

CHAPTER SIX

SHELLY grunted as pain zinged up her shin and the breath was knocked from her body when she fell, landing against something firm. She winced when the IV in her left arm tugged uncomfortably beneath the protective dressing. It took a moment to register she was lying across a very warm, very male body.

Strong, steady arms surrounded her.

"Shelly? Are you all right?" Jared's deep rumbling voice in her ear sent shivers down her spine. On the one hand, she was lucky she'd fallen on an angle, her outstretched hands missing his body and hitting the mattress as she'd fallen. But on the other hand, the position was hardly appropriate, with her breasts squashed partially against Jared's chest.

His bare, muscular chest, her dazed senses realized a heartbeat later. The linens from the hide-a-bed were bunched at his waist, so she could only wonder if the rest of him was just as naked.

Her lower body tingled, ached at the thought.

Thank heavens she'd brushed her teeth in the bathroom and drunk a full glass of water or her breath would have killed Jared on the spot. "Fine. Sorry, I forgot you were there," she whispered.

His chuckle, coming from the darkness that surrounded them, warmed her toes. He shifted on the bed, enough to pull her over so she wasn't sprawled on top of him. Too late, she tried to lever herself upright at the same time so the result was that he inadvertently pulled her hips more firmly against his.

She sucked in a quick breath as an unfamiliar surge of desire streaked south at the intimacy of having the hard length of him snug between her thighs. Her arms melted into limp noodles, unable to keep her upright, until she lowered herself on top of him. Jared must have sensed her weakness as he slid his hands down her back, over her bottom, caressing and pulling her closer.

"Shelly." Her name was a whispered groan, his breath hot against her cheek. Somehow, despite the darkness, his mouth unerringly found hers.

He kissed her gently, chastely, once, then twice, then again, firmer this time, silently begging for more. Unable to resist, she opened to him, responded to his questing tongue, reveling in the heat that sparked between them.

Long-forgotten sensation swamped her. Heat. Passion. Desire. She felt the heat of his kiss down to the soles of her feet. His hands stroked her through her thin sleepshirt. Desperately, she tried to return the favor, her greedy fingers tangling against his chest, following the path of his sculptured muscles, itching to know him more intimately.

Jared reached up to cradle her head, tilting her chin to give him a deeper access to her mouth. Slowly, before she even realized what he was doing, he pulled her down beside him, so the mattress was at her back.

He nuzzled her neck, trailing kisses up along the side of her jaw.

More. She tasted him and longed for more. Had she ever wanted anyone as much as she wanted Jared right now? If she'd felt a fraction of this much need before, she didn't remember. It had been so long since she'd allowed a man to touch her like this. When she felt the rough rasp of his hand sliding upward, under the hem of her sleepshirt, she arched her back, her nipples tightening with eager anticipation.

"Mo-om." A thin wail broke through the red haze of desire. "I need you."

Ty? In a heartbeat, she crashed to earth, to hard-core reality. Shelly instinctively pushed against Jared's shoulders. He didn't try to prevent her from scrambling away, over the edge of the mattress.

"What, Ty?" she called out, pulling her shirt down to cover her bottom as her feet hit the floor. She stumbled down the hall toward her son's room.

Belatedly, she noticed the light shining from the partially open bathroom door.

Her heart sank like a stone. She knew exactly why Ty needed her. Ty had another of his bladder infections, she'd been through too many not to recognize the signs.

"I'm here, honey. It's OK."

"It hurts," he whimpered.

Helplessly, she cradled his shoulders as he stood at the side of the toilet. Although the brightness of the light made her eyes water, she thought perhaps his urine was cloudy again. "Are you finished?"

"Yeah, but make it not hurt." His plea nearly broke her heart.

"I will. Here, I have some medicine for you. Flush the toilet and sit on the cover. Remember those antibiotics the doctor gave us for this? I have an extra bottle." She rummaged in the medicine cabinet as she spoke, finding the bottle and quickly shaking a chewable pill into her hand. "Take this, Ty."

He gamely chewed the medication, used to the routine by now. She offered him a large glass of water to chase the last remnants of medication down.

"Good boy," she praised him. "You drank it all. Ready to go back to bed?"

He nodded and slid off the toilet seat.

Shelly guided him across the hall to his room and into bed. She pulled the covers up and tucked them under his chin. Leaning down, she pressed a soft kiss to his cheek. "I love you, Ty. Try to get some sleep."

"I love you, too." He snuggled down into the pillow. "G'night."

"Good night. Don't let the bedbugs bite." Shelly blinked the moisture from her eyes, a sinking sensation gnawing at her stomach as she stared at his innocent face. Another bladder infection was not a good sign. Mentally she counted backward. How many weeks since his last one? Three or four at the most.

The infections were coming more frequently now. Only the tests would tell them for sure if Ty had renal failure. Shelly stood and tiptoed from his room, closing the door silently behind her. For a moment she stood, shame washing over her. She hadn't heard Ty get up. Almost hadn't heard him call out to her. What was she thinking, kissing Jared like there was no tomorrow?

With a sigh, she covered her flushed face with her cold fingers. She'd momentarily lost her mind, but she had it back now and was determined to keep herself grounded in the present. She hesitated, tempted to sneak back to her own room, avoiding what had nearly happened on the sofa bed by taking the cowardly way out.

"Is Ty all right?" Jared's voice made her jump, sounding suspiciously close. She slapped a hand over her racing heart.

"You scared me." She let out her breath in a rush, then edged away from Ty's door, down the hall toward the living room.

"Did he have a nightmare?"

"No, but he's fine." She kept her voice low, barely above a whisper. She paused near the living room, loath to go any further.

"Good." He came up to stand beside her. The woodsy scent of him teased her nostrils, reminding her of how close they'd just been. "And what about you?"

"Me?" Her voice rose in a squeak.

"Are you all right?"

She knew what he was really asking. Was she ready to pick up where they'd left off? Yes. No. Maybe.

No. Definitely no. "I, um, think we, um, made a mistake," she said in a rush. There, her chest felt lighter already. "I'm sorry, Jared, but I'm not in the market for a relationship."

"I see." He reached out to take her hand, tugged on it, drawing her closer, the warm breath of his mouth dangerously close to her ear. "Can we sit down and talk about this?"

She wanted to. Oh, dear heaven, how she wanted to. But talking to Jared was almost as hazardous as kissing him. He had a way of getting her to reveal too much. His kindness was lethal.

Her starved soul wanted to gobble him up, regardless of the result.

"I don't think so. I need to get some sleep." She resisted the tug of his hand, taking the coward's way out without a blink.

"You must have gotten up originally for some reason," he argued logically, his grip tightening but not painfully so.

Her stomach chose that moment to grumble. She had, in fact, left her bed, what seemed now like hours ago, searching for some toast, hoping her intestinal tract wouldn't veto the bland food.

Another gentle tug on her hand had her stumbling forward, into the living room. To her amazement, and a tiny ridiculous flicker of disappointment, she discovered he'd folded up the sofa bed.

The scene of their passion was no longer in evidence.

"Was that your stomach? Are you hungry?"

"Maybe a little." She rubbed her abdomen. Her

stomach did ache, in the way that told her she could use a little food.

"I'll make you some toast," Jared offered.

"I can make it." Shelly was uncomfortable enough with this strange conversation, moments after their explosive embrace. She couldn't bear for him to wait on her. Crossing the living room, she entered the kitchen, flipping on the small light over her sink.

She was hyper-aware of Jared's presence behind her as she dropped a couple of slices of bread into the toaster.

"Do I need to apologize?" His tone was even, only slightly questioning.

"No." Shelly turned to face him. She was embarrassed by her wanton response to his kiss, but she refused to act like some innocent victim. "Of course not. That…" she waved a hand toward the other room "…obviously shouldn't have happened, but it wasn't your fault."

"'Obviously shouldn't have happened'?" Jared's voice was mild, but she didn't miss the dangerous inflection underlying his tone. "Am I missing something here?"

"No. Yes." She blew out a breath. "I'm saying this badly. I'm attracted to you. That much you've probably figured out by now. But I don't date. Ever. Tyler is too important to me."

Jared's gaze narrowed. "Now I'm really not following you. You dating is bad for Tyler because…?"

She lifted her chin. "Because I won't have him hurt by a relationship that falls apart. He's too young to understand. He sees his friends' parents happily married and automatically will think anyone I date is potential father material.'' When Jared opened his mouth to argue, she lifted a hand to stop him. ''Besides, this isn't only about Ty. It's about me. I'm not ready for this.''

He was silent for a moment. Her bread popped up from the toaster and she decided not to tempt fate by adding butter. Nibbling the dry toast, she watched him.

''Because you're still in love with Ty's father?''

A tiny voice in her head tried to goad her into lying in agreement. But she couldn't do it. Jared had instantly come when she'd called him for help. He'd stayed with her, watched over Ty for her. He was a good man, one who deserved the truth.

''No. I'm not pining for Ty's father. Don't ask me to explain something I'm not sure I completely understand myself,'' she implored with a pleading gaze. ''Trust me, Jared, it's best if we simply go our separate ways. Emotionally, I can't do this. I'm sorry.''

''Me, too.'' Jared stood, his jeans riding low on his hips. She swallowed hard against a lump of dry toast and averted her gaze. ''I'll stay until your last morning dose of antibiotic is in, then I'll be on my way.''

Perversely, she wanted to beg him not to leave. Instead, she forced a smile. ''Thanks for understanding.''

He didn't return her smile but his gaze captured hers. ''I don't think I understand, but call me if you need anything.''

"I will." Her smile faltered, because she knew she wouldn't. Couldn't, or she'd end up back in his arms, begging him to stay.

"I hope so." His expression was grim as he returned to the living room.

Shelly set her toast aside. Her stomach didn't feel any better, but she wasn't certain the nausea had anything to do with her bout of food poisoning. She suspected her illness was because of what she'd just done.

Pushed away the one person who could have been a very good friend.

CHAPTER SEVEN

JARED lay on the sofa, eyes gritty from lack of sleep, watching the sun through Shelly's living-room window as it crept over the horizon. His nerve endings had ceased humming several hours earlier, although his muscles were still tense. He'd only held Shelly close for a few minutes, but his body missed the searing imprint of hers pressed against him, as if they'd been together for days.

He had to stop torturing himself. She wasn't interested, end of story. Bad enough he'd taken advantage of Shelly's weakened condition, what kind of doctor was he anyway? He shifted his weight on the too-soft sofa cushions. The sleeper would have been more comfortable, but he couldn't pull it out. Those stolen moments in time would really haunt him if he did.

When had he ever felt such an intense need to be with a woman? Not just any woman. Kate's pretty smile didn't hold the least bit of appeal. No, only Shelly had the power to drive him insane. Only Shelly possessed the ability to tempt him into forgetting all the reasons why he was too busy to have a life of his own. Only Shelly made him forget about his silent promise to Marc.

He rubbed a weary hand over his eyes. In another hour he could give Shelly her last dose of IV antibiotic, one she was more than capable of giving herself, if he were honest. Then he could leave, his promise having been fulfilled. Today was his scheduled day off and he had a full day of investigating to do. He supposed he should be grateful Shelly had pushed him away. Leigh Wilson was his top priority. Somehow he suspected that he would have blown off his mission at the slightest encouragement from Shelly.

He hadn't imagined her response. Her lips had parted beneath his, her eager hands had stroked his chest, burning his skin, pulling him closer. Her lush body had fitted perfect against him. She wasn't super-slim, all angles and bones like some of the women he'd gone out with. She was soft, full of curves that he'd barely had a chance to see, let alone touch.

Damn. He had to stop thinking about this. Shelly was off limits. She'd told him so herself. She wasn't interested in a relationship and he shouldn't be either. He needed to stop feeling like he'd just lost a best friend. He didn't even know Shelly very well. He couldn't possibly miss her friendship.

Making an abrupt decision, he swung his legs off the couch and levered himself upright. The clock on the wall showed five-thirty, which was close enough to six. He'd hang the last dose of her antibiotic now. No reason to wait.

Shelly was sleeping when he tiptoed into her room. He purposefully kept his gaze averted from her relaxed pose to resist temptation. The IV pole had been pushed off to the side, and he retrieved it and back-filled the mini-bag of medication. When the set-up was complete, he held the end of the IV tubing with one hand and sought the arm that held her IV catheter.

Her hands were curled beneath her cheek. The creamy complexion of her skin drew him closer and his will-power fled as he lightly stroked a finger down the satiny softness. She didn't stir, looking less like the warrior woman he knew her to be. Her features were relaxed, but when she opened her eyes, the green gaze would flash with intense protectiveness toward her son.

Jared mentally smacked himself on the head. He absolutely had to stop mooning over something that would never be. Determined, he gently eased Shelly's right arm out from the covers, thankful she was lying on her left side. Despite the awkward angle, he deftly unwrapped the dressing over her IV, then connected the IV tubing by opening the sliding clamp to a pace that would slowly infuse the medication.

Mission accomplished. Shelly stirred in her sleep, but didn't fully wake up. After double-checking the connection, he backed away. With one last glance at her, he retreated from her room, gently shutting the door behind him.

"Mr Jared?"

He spun around, surprised to hear Ty's voice. He'd tried to get Ty to call him Jared, but Shelly had instilled a certain respect into her son for adults, encouraging the use of Mr or Mrs before their first names.

"Ty. What are you doing up so early?"

"I hafta go to the bathroom. But I'm afraid it's

going to hurt.'' His lower lip trembled as he pulled down the shirt of his pajamas, twisting the fabric in his fingers.

"Hurt?'' Jared hadn't followed Shelly into the bathroom with Ty in the middle of the night. Not only had he needed to grapple with his shredded control, but he'd assumed the boy had just needed some motherly reassurance. He tried to understand what Ty was saying. "You mean, it hurts when you go?''

Ty's brown head nodded up and down. "Yeah. Mom gave me my medicine, but I'm scared.''

"I'll come with you.'' Dazed, Jared gestured for Ty to enter the bathroom ahead of him. "What medication did your mom give you?''

"It's right up there.'' Ty pointed at the medicine cabinet, the mirrored door slightly ajar. Jared swung it open and spied a small brown pharmacy bottle with Ty's name on it.

Chewable Bactrim was printed on the label. Medication used for bladder infections. Ty suffered from bladder infections? He knew exactly what the child was going through. He remembered all too well suffering from a similar malady as a kid.

Jared waited until the boy had finished going to the bathroom—Ty claimed it still hurt but not as badly—then helped him wash his hands. Despite his vow to leave immediately, he ended up making Ty breakfast in the kitchen.

Shelly found them there an hour later. "Good morning.''

"Hi, Mom. Mr Jared made waffles—do you want some?"

"Er, no, thanks. I'll just start with coffee." His heart gave a little pang as she avoided his direct gaze.

"The pot there is fresh. Help yourself." He gestured to the carafe.

"I disconnected the IV because the antibiotic was completely infused," Shelly said as she poured herself a mug of coffee. "Thanks. I didn't hear you come in."

Was there an underlying note of reprimand in her tone? A blind man could have seen she wanted him gone. Out of her house and out of her life.

He set his half-full cup of coffee on the counter. "I didn't want to wake you. But now that you're up, I'll be on my way." He didn't want to go, he wanted to ask about Ty's bladder infection. Did the boy suffer them frequently? Was Ty the one having tests? If so, when? For what? The bladder infections? He opened his mouth, then closed it again, silently turning away.

"Goodbye, Ty, see you later. Hope you're feeling better, Shelly." He made his escape with a minimum of fuss.

Shelly and Ty were a tightly knit family unit. They didn't need him.

Jared took the steps to the courthouse two at a time. Although this was his day off, he should have offered to work after spending his workday with Shelly the day before, but he refused to give in to the guilt. It was time he made some headway on finding Leigh Wilson.

A task much easier said than done. He did look through birth records from the years around when they'd figured Leigh had been born—he guessed she was roughly the same age as Shelly—but his plan of making a list of Wilsons was a daunting one. He tried the tactic of looking for Wilsons who had bought homes in the area about the same time but the list was endless, and he often found himself looking for Bennetts instead. Was Bennett her maiden name or Ty's father's name?

Swearing inwardly, he tried to forget about Shelly and Ty. About the similarities between their situation and Leigh Wilson's. He needed to find Leigh. Should he search only in Milwaukee or try the dozens of outlying suburban cities as well? If he did the latter, his list would quadruple.

Finally, several hours later, armed with reams of paper listing various Wilsons, he gave up and headed to the deli for lunch. Setting the pile of papers beside him, he propped his elbows on the table and rubbed his temples. What was his next step? He had no clue where to go from here.

He tried to study the listing over a sandwich, but the seemingly endless stream of possibilities was daunting. With a shove, he pushed them aside. He needed help. His expertise was keeping kids alive, not investigating lost women. He wasn't skilled enough to do this alone. The last private investigator his dad had hired had failed miserably. But what if he found another, one living right here in town, where he could keep a close eye on him?

Warming to the idea, he turned to the *Yellow Pages*. He interviewed several PIs with specific requests for daily briefings. By the time he got to the last one, the guy stared at the listing of Wilsons while Jared outlined his request then slid them back toward him.

"I understand what you're trying to do, but I think you're going about it all wrong," Samuel Rafter told him.

Jared squashed a flash of impatience. The other two investigators hadn't questioned his means, only assured him they would deliver results. "Oh, really? And just what other option do I have?"

"Start with the birth records," Samuel advised him. "With a full name and a birth date, anyone can be found. But without those two pieces of information, you're spitting in the wind."

"We've looked for a birth date and can't find one."

"Are you sure Leigh is this woman's real first name? I can't tell you how many hours of searching I've done, only to discover that the person goes by their middle name instead of their given first name."

Stunned, Jared stared at him. The idea that Leigh might not be her given first name hadn't occurred to him before now. "I'm not sure," he admitted slowly. "I don't know if the previous guy tried that possibility."

"Look, I've found hundreds of people, performed

hundreds of background investigations. I'll give this a shot. I have access to several databases that private individuals can't get to. But I won't make you any promises. Especially since we don't even know for sure if this Leigh was born here in Milwaukee.''

Just that simply, Jared made his decision. "Go ahead and try. I'll pay the initial fee, and the balance when you find her."

Samuel nodded. "Great. Thanks."

Jared wrote out a check, then stood. After a moment's hesitation, he sat back down. Completely ignoring the sharp stab of guilt that pierced the space between his shoulder blades, he asked, "How much extra to do a simple background investigation on someone?"

Samuel named his price. Jared nodded, then reached for his checkbook again. As much as he didn't have any right to pry into Shelly's personal life, he knew he couldn't focus his attention on Leigh until he'd discovered the truth about Shelly. "Then I'd like you to do a background investigation on Shelly Bennett."

CHAPTER EIGHT

SHELLY gritted her teeth and paced the length of her kitchen while the pediatrician's office put her on hold for the third time. Today was Tuesday. Ty was due home from school any moment and she still didn't know if they were supposed to go in for his tests the following morning or not. After what seemed like eons, the nurse came back on the line.

"Ms Bennett? Dr Delaney asked that your son's tests be delayed until he finishes his course of antibiotics."

"But that won't be until Friday." And she'd already scheduled her work hours around the previously scheduled tests. She was off tonight, but was scheduled to work Thursday night on the 7 p.m. to 7 a.m. shift, which meant she'd be in bad shape to take Ty in the next day. "Will two days really make any difference? Is there any way I can talk to Dr Delaney myself?"

"Not until much later tonight. This place is crawling with sick kids. I'll ask him to give you a call when he's finished seeing patients." The woman's tone wasn't encouraging.

"Thank you." Shelly blew out an exasperated breath and replaced her cordless phone in the charger. If she waited too long, and wasn't able to change the doctor's mind, she'd be stuck. There was no choice but to go into work and examine the schedule. Maybe she could ask Kristin or Jess to switch days with her.

Tyler was doing great on the antibiotics, but she wanted these renal function tests over with. She needed to know exactly what future hardships Ty might face. The not knowing day after day was more difficult than hearing definitive news, one way or the other.

"Hi, Mom!" Ty dashed into the house, dropping his book bag carelessly on the floor as he rushed over to give her a hug. "Guess what? I got a star on my story paper."

"You did?" Shelly grinned as Ty bubbled over with excitement. "Let me see."

"It's in my bag. I'm hungry, can I have a snack?"

Ty was a whirlwind of energy. Shelly knew from past experience to let him eat first, then discuss homework. Not that the kindergarten teacher often gave much in the way of homework other than the standard nightly reading session that she and Ty enjoyed so that it hardly counted.

She busied herself with setting out Ty's snack, then glanced at the clock. There was time to run over to Lifeline before dinner.

"Can we have Mr Jared over for dinner?" Ty asked, dipping his slice of apple in the caramel and taking a big bite. "Please?"

Shelly was running out of excuses to give him. Ty had grown attached to Jared in the short time he'd watched over her son. Five days had passed since her bout of food poisoning and she'd only seen Jared in passing. Yet he'd taken up residence in the back of her mind. During the darkest hours of the night, she replayed the kiss over and over again, until she could scream with frustration. Sometimes she imagined what could have happened if she hadn't chickened out. If she'd put Ty back to bed, then gone back to the living room so they could pick up their love-making where they'd left off.

Each time Ty brought up the subject of Jared, though, she knew she'd made the right decision in letting him go. Look how attached her son had grown after a few measly hours. She couldn't bear to imagine what might happen if she'd allowed herself to get really tangled up with Jared and the affair had ended after several weeks.

Marc had died before Ty had been born, so her son hadn't felt the acute loss of his father. She had no idea how Ty would react to losing a father figure now that he was old enough to understand the impact.

In an effort to keep busy, she took Tyler with her to Lifeline to check out the schedule. Sure enough, Kristin was scheduled to fly the night shift Wednesday night. Ty went over to talk to Reese, who cheerfully fed her son's eager questions about flying while she dialed Kristin's number.

Kristin was willing to switch shifts, Wednesday for Thursday, to Shelly's relief. When she went in search of Ty, she found him with Jared, who was dressed in street clothes, instead of his usual flight suit. Apparently he wasn't working.

"Hi, Shelly." Was it her imagination or did his gaze hold a hint of longing? "How are you feeling?"

"Much better, thanks." Because of her illness, her work days had gotten off track so she hadn't flown as much with Jared as she had originally been scheduled to. And now she'd changed her next shift, too. Fate was obviously giving her a helping hand in avoiding Jared, as if divine intervention was reinforcing that her decision to stay away from him was the right one.

"Mom, Mr Jared said he'd love to have dinner with us." Ty swirled and dipped a small toy helicopter, one Reese must have given to him.

Her eyes widened with dismay. "Ty, I didn't pull anything out for dinner. I thought we'd stop on the way home and get something."

"There's a restaurant down the highway a bit that caters for families." Jared's smile didn't quite reach his eyes and she hid a wince. He obviously sensed how much she dreaded spending time with him. Not because he wasn't good company, but simply so she didn't have a constant reminder of how things could be different.

"Jared?" Kate poked her head out of the debriefing room. "Dr Evans called and asked if you would mind working his night shift tonight and tomorrow night. His wife just went into labor."

Saved by the birthing mother, Shelly thought with relief as Jared nodded. "Of course. He warned me her time was near. Tell him to let us know how things go."

"I will." Kate ducked back out.

"Sorry, Ty. I guess we'll have to make this another time." Jared smiled and placed his hand on Ty's shoulder. "Take care and listen to your mom, OK?"

"I will." Ty was disappointed, but he seemed to understand as they left the hangar. To make up for it, and to ease her conscience, Shelly took him to the family restaurant Jared had suggested. Ty appreciated the kid-friendly atmosphere, but she sensed he would have enjoyed himself much more if Jared had come along with them.

That night, Ty included Jared in his nightly prayers and Shelly felt the fissure in her heart widen. Her son missed having a father figure in his life and she was at a loss as to what to do about it.

When she was alone in her room later, she took out her journal.

Marc, there are thousands of single mothers in the world raising children on their own, but how do they manage to make up for the absence of a father? I can't bear the thought of Ty being hurt, but at the same time he clearly yearns for a male role model to look up to.

Then there's the small matter of his potential illness. Even if I found someone I could fall in love with, someone I could imagine spending the rest of my life with, is that really fair when Ty's road to health will likely be filled with rocks the size of boulders? Even the strongest of marriages have caved under that sort of pressure.

*I want to give Ty the best chance at a normal life,
but at what emotional cost? Is it better for Ty to
live without a father or to have a father that he
loves, then loses? Neither option is acceptable, yet
it's a decision I could be forced to make.*
    Shelly.

The next night, she left Ty with his friend Alex and
headed into work. When she saw Jared seated in the
debriefing room, she remembered he was covering for
Rick Evans.

"So what's the news on Mrs Evans?" she asked
as she helped herself to a cup of coffee. Night shifts
were wicked on her sleep cycle. She'd tried to take a
nap earlier while Ty was in school, but hadn't been
able to sleep.

"Baby girl, Clarise Marie Evans, 8 pounds, 2
ounces." Jared gestured at the bulletin board where
the baby pool was posted. "Guess what? You won
fifty dollars in the birth-date pool."

"I did? Wow. That will help me pay for a new hot-
water heater. Maybe I'll buy a lottery ticket," she
joked.

Jared frowned and was about to say something
when their pilot, Dirk, came into the room and began
to start the debriefing.

She didn't have time to wonder what Jared had
been about to say because shortly after report, their
first call came in.

"Seven-year-old needing an ICU-to-ICU transfer
to Children's Memorial. He's highest on the list for

a liver transplant and they have a match.'' Shelly read the message out loud.

''Let's go.''

Dirk had just finished telling them the weather report was good, so they simply grabbed their gear and made their way to the chopper. Once airborne, Shelly listened as Dirk went over the flight plan with the base.

Luckily, the hospital wasn't far, only a thirty-minute flight. Shelly remembered once flying seven hours to Michigan to pick up a patient who'd needed to come to Children's Memorial for a transplant. With every breath she took, she was aware of Jared sitting beside her. She couldn't imagine sitting next to him for a fourteen-hour round trip. Small doses of him were hard enough. Fourteen hours and her nerves would be shot.

Shelly kept her attention focused on the view out the window, although the chances of geese flying at night were nonexistent. Still, her job was to help the pilot keep an eye out for any flight hazards, and if that meant staring out the window instead of talking to Jared, then that's exactly what she'd do.

As if he sensed her reluctance to communicate, Jared kept silent as well. Or maybe he was angry with her, although he'd greeted her nicely enough. Strange, though, the way he'd seemed willing, almost anxious to go to dinner when Ty had asked.

''ETA five minutes,'' Dirk announced through the headset.

''Roger that.'' Shelly pulled the flight bag toward

her and double-checked the equipment. The shift prior to theirs should have restocked the bag, but she wanted to make sure. If something critical was missing, they could possibly replenish the supplies from the hospital.

"Prepare to land." Dirk was older than Reese, with many more flight hours logged under his belt, but in her opinion his landing wasn't as smooth.

She and Jared disembarked from the helicopter and wheeled the gurney inside. Their patient, Ethan Adams, lay listlessly in his bed. His skin was an eerie shade of orange—Shelly was shocked at how jaundiced he was.

His mother sat beside him, her expression sad but hopeful. Shelly flashed the woman a reassuring smile as she approached the bedside.

"Hi, Ethan. We're here to take you to Children's Memorial." Shelly covered his thin arm with her hand. "Have you ever flown in a helicopter before?"

Ethan turned his head toward her and she wanted to weep when she realized how sick he was. His breathing was shallow, his pulse too high. Even the whites of his eyes were yellow. "No." His voice was pathetically weak.

"Well, you're in for a treat." She had to push the words past her constricted throat. Dear God, he looked so awful, she could only imagine how much worse he must feel. While she talked, she quickly switched over the lines and tubes to their portable monitor while Jared spoke to the transferring physician. "You'll be able to tell all your friends how you flew in the Lifeline helicopter."

"Won't they be jealous?" his mom gamely added.

The barest hint of a smile tugged at the corner of Ethan's dry, cracked lips. Shelly wondered how long he'd been waiting for a liver transplant. Obviously, too long. She swallowed hard. Would this be Tyler in a few years, too sick to move as he waited for his kidney transplant?

Don't do this to yourself, she warned. Tyler doesn't have liver failure. Dialysis wasn't the greatest option in the world, but it was at least a feasible bridge to a transplant. Ethan, bless his heart, didn't have even that much of a chance. There was no artificial bridge to a new liver. This little boy needed a liver transplant or he would die.

She wondered if Ethan's mother knew how serious the situation was. By the hopeful expression in the woman's eyes, she wasn't certain. Surgery in and of itself was always a risk. Anesthesia, bleeding, infection—the complications were endless. And once he made it through surgery, he'd have to take a boatload of medication to keep his body from rejecting the new organ. All transplant patients, whether heart, lung, liver or kidney, had to take the same anti-rejection medication.

Her fingers fumbled with the non-invasive blood-pressure tubing and she blinked, trying to focus. Jared reached around her and gently took the tubing from her limp hands.

"Here. I can do this." His voice was kind, gentle, as if he sensed her inner turmoil.

Her smile of thanks was brittle. She longed to lean on him, to verbalize her worst fears, but this wasn't the time or the place. Ethan needed to be transported. This transplant was his only chance to live long enough to see his eighth birthday.

"Ready?" Jared asked her. She nodded. "Let's go."

Jared told Ethan's mother they would meet her at Children's Memorial, reinforcing the rule against parents riding along. Shelly barely listened. She gazed down at Ethan, but sometimes his features blurred, resembling her son, Ty.

Inside the helicopter, years of training took over. Shelly placed the patient headphones over Ethan's ears, then pushed the button on her microphone. "Can you hear me?"

The boy's yellow eyes widened and he nodded. She smiled. "Good. If you need anything, just tell us. We can hear you, too. First, we need to listen for a minute until the pilot takes off."

"Ready for takeoff," Dirk intoned over the intercom.

"We're good to go back here," Jared responded.

Ethan seemed to enjoy the flight, and after they reached their cruising altitude, Shelly helped prop up his shoulders so he could look out the window.

"The lights are beautiful," he whispered.

Shelly gently squeezed his bony shoulders, her

heart breaking at how thin and weak he was. "Yes, they are," she agreed softly.

Luckily, the biggest problem Ethan had during the ride was a mild bout of air-sickness. Jared gave him Compazine in his IV to combat the nausea. Although Ethan was physiologically stable during the entire flight, Shelly couldn't erase the comparisons to Ty from her mind.

"ETA ten minutes," Dirk warned them.

Shelly told Ethan that they were getting close to landing and explained how they'd then get to the ICU. What she didn't say was that the flight was the easy part.

Ethan still had a long surgical procedure and recovery to get through before he was out of the woods. She prayed he'd survive long enough to brag to all his friends about his Lifeline flight.

During the flight to Children's Memorial, Jared watched Shelly nearly as closely as he did their patient. Something was wrong. She wasn't her usual self. She seemed distracted, almost mentally absent at times. Just at the point he was seriously considering grounding her from flying, she quickly picked up on a subtle change in Ethan's status as they were about to land.

"His breathing is worse, I just noticed a five-second pause between breaths. His pulse ox is OK, but I suspect he's retaining carbon dioxide. I think he'll need to be intubated and I don't think we should wait until we get to the PICU." As she spoke, she withdrew the necessary equipment from the flight bag.

Jared nodded his agreement. They only had about five minutes until landing, but if they waited too long, they'd be performing the procedure in the elevator. Better to do it now, when they were in a controlled environment, with equipment readily available.

"Dirk, make it a smooth approach. We're intubating back here. Shelly, hand me the laryngoscope and give him a half-milligram of Versed."

Shelly gave the medication, then passed the instrument into Jared's hands. He visualized the back of Ethan's throat with the 'scope, then proceeded to place the breathing tube. He verified placement with a device on the end of the tube while Shelly inflated the cuff and then taped the airway in place.

"ETA, one minute," Dirk informed them.

They landed without incident and quickly took Ethan to the PICU. There, they ordered a chest X ray to make sure the breathing tube they'd placed was indeed in the right place. The doctor there also ordered a blood gas to see how high Ethan's carbon dioxide level was.

He was relieved to discover Ethan's carbon dioxide level was higher than normal, verifying that intubation had been necessary. He would have felt bad if the results had been normal. Shelly seemed loath to leave Ethan, but their pagers went off, indicating another call.

They were back up in the air with Dirk for a good

fifteen minutes when their call was canceled. Dirk banked and headed back to the Lifeline hangar.

"Lifeline to base, why was the transport canceled?" Jared asked. They had been called to transfer a severely premature newborn baby to the neonatal ICU at Children's Memorial.

"Apparently the patient took a turn for the worse. Survival at this point is questionable so transport was aborted."

"Roger that, ten-four."

Shelly continued to exist in her own world when they returned to the hangar. Jared followed her into the lounge.

"What's wrong?" He didn't tap-dance around the issue; the next call out could come at any moment. "You're not in any condition to fly."

"What?" A green spark flared in Shelly's eyes and she straightened her shoulders. He wanted to applaud with approval at her reaction. "Of course I can fly. Why do you think something's wrong?"

"You've been seriously preoccupied since we responded to Ethan's call. I wasn't sure who I needed to worry about more, you or Ethan." Jared gestured for her to sit on the sofa. "Talk to me. Are you worried about Ty?"

"I— Yes." Shelly momentarily rubbed her eyes. "I'm fine to fly, honest. I'm just a little worried about Ty. He has several tests scheduled for Friday morning."

Pleased with her admission, he gentled his tone. "What sort of tests? I know he had a bladder infection a few days ago, but that's not totally uncommon in kids. Heck, I had a series of bladder infections when I was young.''

''You did?'' Her eyes widened with interest. ''What happened? Did you finally grow out of them?''

''Yeah. My right ureter was crooked when I was born, but as I grew older it straightened out and the infections stopped.'' He reached over and took Shelly's hand. ''I'll come with you for Ty's tests if you like.''

She didn't answer right away, but stared down at their clasped hands. He ached to pull her into his arms. When she spoke, her voice was so low he had to strain to listen.

''I suspect Ty's problems are more serious than that. During his last routine check-up at the pediatrician's office, his lab values were on the high side, toward abnormal. Based on his history with the bladder infections, the doctor recommended these additional tests. Seeing Ethan so sick, waiting for a transplant, was sort of like visualizing Ty's worst-case scenario.''

''Shelly, as a nurse I can understand why you're thinking the worst. But you also know that the chances are good that Ty will be fine.'' His thumb stroked the back of her hand. Her skin was soft, he remembered their embrace as if it were yesterday. She'd haunted him in the days they'd been apart. He'd missed her, more than he'd thought possible. Had she missed him at all? He suspected not. The

Wonderwoman image returned. She was so strong, one of the strongest women he'd ever known.

"I know, but with his creatinine on the high side, it's hard not to suspect the worst. Lately, being surrounded by these sick kids has started to bother me. Maybe I need a career change."

"Don't jump into anything yet." Jared tried not to show his panic. Shelly was a great peds nurse, one he'd hate to lose. "Sick kids are always more difficult to care for, that's why they're so rewarding."

"I know, but you said yourself I was distracted," she pointed out.

"Yes. But you also picked up on Ethan's respiratory status change. You're a good nurse, Shelly. Don't be so hard on yourself. Maybe you'll feel better once Ty has had his tests. I'd really like to be there for you on Friday."

"Thanks, but that isn't necessary." Shelly gave his hand a slight squeeze, then gently pulled away. He tried not to grind his teeth in frustration. Why was she so determined to do everything alone? Why couldn't she accept his support, even as a friend?

Or his support as more than a friend?

"I care about Ty, too." He tried to make her understand. She held herself aloof, but he craved so much more. "Will you at least call me when his test results come back?"

"I— Yes. I'll call you with his results." She sent him a confused look. "I didn't realize you two were so close. Ty talks about you all the time."

"He does?" Jared couldn't prevent a broad smile.

"Ty is a great kid, Shelly, but, of course, you already knew that. I liked spending time with him. Having a masculine influence in his life certainly couldn't hurt."

"Oh, really?" Green flames sparked from her eyes and she jumped up from her seat beside him, planting her hands on her hips. It was a sign of his total madness that he wanted to grab those hips, pull her close and kiss the heck out of her, not the least put off by her annoyance. "And I suppose you're offering to take on that role? Thanks, but no thanks. I know what's best for my son. For your information, I recently enrolled him in a big brothers-big sisters program. He has a male role model. One I don't need to get involved with."

She spun on her heel and stalked off, toward the vending machines located on the other side of the room. Jared let her go. He hadn't meant to offer to be Ty's father figure, but the more he thought about it, the more he warmed to the idea. Of course, he should have known Wonderwoman had already taken matters into her own hands.

After the end of his shift, Jared stayed in his office for a couple of hours to get some paperwork done. The private investigator he'd hired to do the background check was due to report in at nine. Elbows propped on his desk, Jared held his head in his hands, fighting exhaustion.

When the phone rang, he jerked awake. Groggy and half-asleep, he picked up the phone. "Dr O'Connor."

"Samuel Rafter here. I have some interesting news regarding Shelly Bennett's background check."

"Really?" His sleepiness evaporated. Still, he hesitated. Shelly would be furious if she ever found out he'd pried into her personal life, something he had no right to do. Still, he had to know. "What is it?"

"Shelly Bennett didn't exist up until six years ago, when she moved to Milwaukee and formally changed her name. Her original name was Sharon Leigh Wilson." The PI paused, then continued, "She's the woman you've hired me to find."

CHAPTER NINE

STUNNED, Jared blinked. It took several moments for the PI's words to seep into his brain.

"Shelly is Leigh Wilson? Ty is my nephew?"

"Yes. Sharon legally changed her name six years ago to Shelly Bennett. Bennett is her mother's maiden name. I have to tell you, I would never have found her so easily without your request for a background check on Shelly Bennett."

Jared barely heard him. He still couldn't quite grasp the news. He'd found Leigh. Leigh was Shelly. Ty was his nephew. He wanted to stand up and shout for the whole world to hear. *Ty was his nephew!* Good grief, he needed to call his parents. He had to let them know he found Marc's son.

"Want me to dig further?" Samuel was saying now.

"Huh? No, that's OK. I really don't need to know anything else."

"If you're sure. I did find out that Shelly is legally a nurse in the state of Wisconsin. She changed her name prior to graduating from nursing school. If you had known she was a nurse, we could have found her a long time ago through the State Board."

If his father had hired a decent private investigator, they would have known about Shelly a long time ago, too, but that was in the past. Right now, Jared was more concerned about the future. They'd found her at last.

"Thanks, Samuel. I'll send the balance of your fee today. You've more than earned it."

Jared hung up the phone, then dialed his parents. Heck, the hour was early, especially considering the Eastern time zone difference but he didn't think they'd mind. Not when he told them the news.

His mother answered the phone.

"Mom, are you sitting down?"

"Why, do you have bad news for me?" His mother sounded uncertain.

"Good news. I have really good news for you. But you'd better sit down to hear this."

"Oh, dear." Her voice grew faint and he imagined his mother sinking bonelessly into a kitchen chair. "Are you telling me what I think you're telling me?"

Jared had to smile. "Yes. I found her. Leigh Wilson has changed her name to Shelly Bennett and she has a son, Tyler. I found Marc's son."

His mother burst into tears. Jared had expected the reaction, but hearing her heartfelt sobs a thousand miles away, and unable to comfort her, shook him anyway. "Really? Have you seen him? Does he look like Marc?"

"Yes, I've seen him and he looks just like Marc." Jared could easily remember how the very similar facial expressions Ty used mirrored his brother's. Why hadn't he known on some instinctive level that Tyler shared his blood? Maybe because Ty's beautiful mother had clouded his vision, ruining his concentration.

"When can we meet him?" his mother demanded. "How soon can you bring him out?"

Whoa, things were moving a little quicker than Jared had planned. He quickly backpedaled. "Soon, Mom, I promise. I've seen Tyler for myself but he doesn't know about you and Dad yet. In fact, Shelly doesn't know that I'm aware of her real identity."

"I don't care what it takes, Jared, we want to see Ty. As soon as humanly possible. She's kept him from us long enough."

Jared was taken aback by the hard edge to her tone, then realized that she was probably worried because of his dad's health. "I promise, Mom, you and Dad will get to see him soon. Give me a few days here to talk to Shelly. I'm sure she'll be reasonable. Now, take care. I'll be in touch soon."

He hung up the phone, then sat back in his chair. Exhausted, he struggled to think clearly. Shelly was certainly a reasonable person, she didn't seem the type to isolate Ty from his family. Yet wasn't that exactly what she'd done? Six years ago, pregnant with his brother's child, she'd run from Boston to hide in Milwaukee. She'd gone as far as to legally change her name, making it difficult to find her. Why had she felt such drastic steps had been necessary? Had she been so freaked out by the pregnancy that she'd wanted to hide where no one knew her? Had she been ashamed to find herself pregnant without the benefit of marriage?

He dug the heels of his hands into his eyes, trying to think straight. There was only one way to know for sure what had gone through her mind all those years ago and that was to ask Shelly herself. But right now that wasn't an option. She was sleeping.

Something he should be doing. Jared pushed back from his desk, then remembered he needed to pay Samuel the remainder of his fee. After quickly taking care of that detail, he headed home.

All he needed was a few hours of sleep, then he'd go and see Shelly. His timing sucked, he knew darn well Ty was scheduled for his tests first thing in the morning, but this couldn't wait. His parents had dreamed about seeing their lost grandchild for six years and his father's health was tenuous at best.

As far as he was concerned, he agreed with his mother. They'd waited long enough.

Jared barely managed to sleep for three hours, before the ringing phone woke him up. He grabbed it a second too late. Whoever was on the other end had already hung up.

Damn. He set the receiver back in its cradle and flopped back down on the bed. The night of Marc's death had replayed itself over and over in his dreams. What if he'd handled that night differently? He knew deep in his gut that if they hadn't fought, Marc wouldn't have stormed off in anger. Jared hadn't found out until reading the autopsy report that Marc had been drinking, too. No, Jared hadn't even bothered to really listen to what his brother had been saying that night. He'd been too busy studying for his pediatric boards, the ones he'd been due to take early the next morning, and had been more than a little annoyed with Marc for daring to interrupt.

He closed his eyes and groaned. He'd take that moment of irritation back if he could. He'd already taken the whole evening and replayed the events, always with a different ending. Marc didn't storm off in anger to slam his car against a concrete highway divider, but instead they talked until Marc fell asleep on his sofa, spending the night safe in Jared's apartment.

Good grief, there was so much he needed to make up for. He hadn't just lost a brother that night, his parents had lost a son, Shelly had lost her fiancé and Tyler his father. So much loss from his stupid action.

Shelly's face hovered in his mind and the impact of her true identity hit him hard. Shelly had loved Marc. She'd been intimate with him. Created a baby with him. A flash of jealousy caught him off guard. Damn, he couldn't close his eyes without imagining the two of them together.

Shelly and Marc. Marc and Shelly. Marc making love to Shelly…

The phone rang again. This time he pulled himself upright in time to answer it.

"Yeah?" He didn't care if he sounded rude. So help him, if he heard a telemarketer's voice on the other end of the line, rude wouldn't begin to describe his reaction.

"Dr O'Connor? This is Dr Jacobs, your father's cardiologist. I need your help."

Jared frowned and sat up on the edge of his bed. He'd spoken to the cardiologist several times over the past few weeks, getting regular updates on his father's condition.

"My help? With what?"

"Your father is making arrangements to fly to Milwaukee, against my advice. At the very least, I'd like him to undergo another echocardiogram before he travels. But he's refusing treatment at this time."

Refusing treatment? Traveling to Milwaukee? Jared wanted to bang his head against the wall, because surely that would make the sledgehammer in his head stop. "I'll talk to him."

"You'd better hurry," Dr Jacobs advised. "Because I believe he's planning to book the next available flight."

Shelly tossed and turned the entire night before Ty's tests. Partially, she was sure, because her sleep schedule was totally screwed up working the night shift. But deep down she also couldn't help but worry about what the day would bring. In a few hours she should know if Ty needed additional testing or if his kidney function was normal.

Twice she'd picked up her journal, only to set it back down without writing a word. She wasn't in the mood to write. The words simply wouldn't come. And she was tired of one-sided conversations with Marc. As much as she'd once loved the freedom of spilling her thoughts on paper, she now had to battle the insane urge to call Jared. He would understand her concern, her inability to sleep. He was the only other person who would care, one way or the other. Heck, he'd offered to go with her to the tests. Why had she been so stubborn as to refuse?

She stared blankly up at the ceiling. Jared was a great guy. She respected his expertise as a doctor, yet he didn't have the barest hint of the kind of arrogance she'd come to expect from the physicians she worked with. He listened to her, sensed her moods before she understood them herself. He'd dropped everything to help her out when she'd been sick.

And the man definitely knew how to kiss.

The minute he stepped within arm's reach, her nerve endings tingled with awareness. She couldn't remember ever being so in tune with another person. Intimacy, or lack thereof, had been easy to avoid since losing Marc. She hadn't been interested in other men. In being close to them. In sharing her life with them.

Until she'd met Jared.

That was the biggest problem of all. Silently, she forced herself to acknowledge the truth. Her feelings for Jared went much deeper than simple attraction. From the very beginning, she'd been drawn to him. She didn't know if it was his internal strength, his innate sense of honesty, his ability to read her so clearly or a combination of all three that had sucked her in, but she was definitely hooked.

Telling him about Ty's illness had been liberating. He'd held her hand, caressed the back of it with his thumb. And she'd felt so connected to him on a deeper, subliminal level. An experience she'd never felt with anyone, even Marc. She'd cared for Marc, but what she felt with Jared was so very different from the simple fun she'd shared with Marc that she wasn't sure of anything now.

She'd pulled away from Jared, afraid of her strange response, but now she regretted her action. Everything had seemed so confusing, so different. She didn't understand her own emotions.

Still didn't. Except for one simple fact. She wanted to see Jared. Needed to see him. To talk to him about her fears over Ty's tests. Just to hear his deep, reassuring voice. Was it too early to call?

Her alarm jangled and she flew upright, slamming her fist on top of the clock for silence. Maybe after she showered and dressed, just before she left for the hospital, she'd call Jared. If nothing else, just hearing his voice, if he was too busy to rearrange his schedule at the last minute, would help cheer her up.

An hour later, she gathered her courage and dialed his number. After several rings of the phone, his answering-machine kicked in. He'd left his pager number on the recording, so she quickly—before she could chicken out and change her mind—tried that number too.

But by the time she and Ty were ready to leave for the hospital, Jared hadn't returned her call.

Waiting was a killer. How did families put up with this every day? She worked in the medical field and still couldn't stand watching the seconds tick away into longer minutes.

Finally, Tyler was finished with his tests. Eagerly, she waited for the doctor to come and see her.

"Ms Bennett? I'm Dr Arlando. So far, Ty's preliminary test results look good, but the radiologist still needs to do the final reading. I'm afraid he won't get to that until later today."

"Like how much later?" She didn't bother to hide her dismay.

"Well." He shrugged. "By the end of the day, I suppose."

Four hours? This man actually expected her to wait another four interminable, potentially life-altering hours?

"Can't you put a rush on this? Please?" She clutched his arm in a desperate grip. "We've been waiting for weeks. I need to know these results."

"I'll see what we can do." He patted her hand as if she were a small child, then turned and walked away.

Shelly curled her fingers into fists as she watched him go. Four more hours. How would she stand it?

Rather than head home, Shelly stopped at Ty's favorite fast-food joint for lunch, then headed to the park for an impromptu picnic. Tyler was oblivious to her concern, enjoying himself on the play-set. When she'd looked at her watch for the tenth time in as many minutes, she ripped it off her wrist in exasperation and stuffed it in the pocket of her jeans.

Don't think the worst, she lectured herself sternly.

Hadn't Arlando mentioned the preliminary tests looked good? Why not look on the bright side? That was already a good sign. Shelly tipped her face to the sun, enjoying the warmth against her skin. For the first time in weeks, a tiny flame of hope flickered in her heart. She and Ty could stop at the store on the way home, pick up some cake and ice cream to prepare for a celebration. She'd call Jared, invite him, too.

Shelly pushed Tyler on the swings, grinning as he squealed in delight. Then she purposefully took her time going to the grocery store, then to the drugstore, to pick up some personal items before finally heading home.

The light on her answering-machine was blinking. With a rush, she dashed over and pushed the button.

"Shelly? Jared here. I'd really like to talk to you. Please, call me when you get in."

She blushed at the wave of pleasure that washed over her at the husky sound of his voice, then played it again, saving the message instead of erasing it. He hadn't mentioned getting her messages, but maybe he was trying to spare her the embarrassment. She tapped her fingers on the counter, debating whether or not to call. Nah, there was no point in calling now, she'd wait until Ty's final test results were in.

The doctor didn't call until almost half past five. But when he did, the call was brief.

"All Tyler's kidney function test results are perfectly normal."

Normal! Her son's kidney function was *normal*.

With a war-whoop, she slammed down the phone and let loose with a wild dance around her kitchen.

Ty was fine. Healthy and fine. Whoo-hoo, Ty was healthy and fine.

"Mom?" Her son slanted her an odd look. "Are you going crazy?"

She dropped her head back and laughed a true, heartfelt laugh of pure relief. "Yep. I'm crazy, Ty. I'm crazy—giddy with happiness."

He scrunched up his face. "What's giddy?"

"Me. I'm giddy. We're going to celebrate. Let's find our party hats." She grabbed his hand and tugged him down the hall and into her room.

"Is it my birthday?" Ty asked doubtfully, when she found the old box of New Year's party hats and noise-makers and immediately plopped a hat on his head, then took a party horn and blew it loudly in his face. "I'm six years old?"

"Nope, it's not your birthday. Or mine either," she added when she saw him open his mouth again. She knew Ty didn't have a clue as to the seriousness of the tests, but there was no one else to celebrate with. "I just feel like having a party."

Jared. Her eyes widened and she hefted the box of party favors on her hip, intent on heading back into the kitchen. Now was the perfect time to call Jared. He'd understand her excitement.

But once again he didn't answer his phone. She couldn't bring herself to leave a message, but figured she'd try again later.

Determined to have fun, Shelly put a CD in her

portable player and grabbed Ty's hand. "Come on, buster, let's dance."

Ty didn't need any encouragement. He eagerly joined in her enthusiastic swaying and singing along with the song.

"Celebrate, celebrate…"

"Mom!" Ty blew his horn in her face to get her attention. "Someone's at the door."

"Really?" She turned the music down a few notches, then danced over to the door. Her heartbeat tripled when she saw Jared standing there.

"Hi!" She flashed him a broad smile, opening the door wider. "Come on in! You're just in time for cake and ice cream."

"Hi, yourself." Jared raised his eyebrows when she stuck the noise-maker in her mouth and blew it at his nose. "Whose birthday is it?"

"No one's birthday, silly," she chided him. "We're celebrating Ty's kidney function test results. All normal!" She spun in a little circle, shuffling her feet to the beat. "Grab yourself a hat and join the fun."

"Shelly." He grabbed her arm before she could dance off, and clasped her to him in a quick hug. "I'm so happy to hear about Ty's tests."

"Mr Jared!" Tyler ran up and flung his arms around Jared's long legs before she could respond. "I'm glad you came to our party."

"Me, too." Shelly's eyes misted when Jared leaned down to include her son in their embrace. "It's good to see you."

"Want some cake? And some neo—neopol—what kind of ice cream, Mom?"

"Neapolitan," Shelly corrected.

"Yeah, Neapolitan ice cream," Ty echoed. "It's got three flavors."

"Sure. Why not?"

"First you have to put on your party hat." Shelly plopped a neon-blue hat on his head, thinking his eyes were a much prettier blue. "And here's your noise-maker."

Jared gamely played along as they stuffed themselves with cake and ice cream. Then, in keeping with their backward celebration, they decided to eat dinner, which consisted of burgers cooked on the small charcoal grill outside.

Finally, the hour grew late enough for Ty to go to bed. Shelly was thrilled that Jared didn't make up some excuse to leave. He'd mentioned wanting to talk, but she was interested in something more.

She'd learned an amazing thing today. Exciting news was a hundred times better when you shared it with someone. And if the unthinkable had happened, if she had been told bad news, then maybe she would have been able to deal with it better if she'd shared that with Jared too. Maybe, just maybe, she didn't have to do everything alone.

"I'll just be a few minutes," she murmured to Jared as she guided Ty into his room.

"I know." Jared leaned down to pick up the dirty dishes. "I'll be here."

"I know." She flashed him an impish grin. Ty

dawdled in the bathroom, then again when he wanted a bedtime story. Shelly leaned down and firmly kissed his cheek.

"I love you, Ty, but how about if I read you two stories tomorrow night instead? I need to clean up the mess from the party." Flimsy excuse but, hey, he was only five. He couldn't know the real reason she wanted to get back to Jared.

"OK. Good night." He snuggled down in his bed, then two seconds later his eyes popped back open. "Almost forgot to say my prayers."

Shelly rolled her eyes while her son quickly went through his nightly ritual. She didn't even mind when he added Jared to his prayer listing again. She gave him another hug and a kiss, her heart bursting with love as he kissed her cheek again.

She detoured into the bathroom, hesitated for a minute, then opened the box of condoms in her medicine cabinet. The box had been among the list of personal items she'd bought earlier that day. Would Jared think she was some sort of loose woman for buying them? She could tell him she hadn't been with a man since the night Ty had been conceived, but he might think there was something wrong with her. After a ping-pong internal debate, she pocketed the packet and returned to the kitchen.

True to his word, Jared was in the process of clearing away the mess.

"Leave them, I'll take care of it later."

Jared turned toward her, his gaze so intense her

breath caught in her throat. "You shouldn't have to clean up everything alone."

"I'm not alone." And she'd never been so happy to admit it. The condom she'd grabbed from the bathroom burned a hole in her pocket. She licked her dry lips. "You're here. Have I told you how happy I am to see you?"

His blue eyes darkened when she approached. He stared at her mouth as if completely fascinated. "No, I don't think you did."

"Hmm. My mistake." She stepped closer, and his arms came up automatically to pull her into his embrace. Leaning up, she pressed her lips against the square line of his jaw, enjoying his salty taste. "I'm so glad you came. I needed to celebrate with you tonight."

"I'm happy to help." His voice was deep and rough, like coarse sandpaper. "Shelly—"

"Shh." She wrapped her arms around his neck, pulling his head down to hers. This time her kiss found his mouth. In a heartbeat he yanked her hips against his, crushing her breasts against his chest, deepening the kiss.

Yes! Her senses soared, all logical thought dissipating like mist. Dear God, yes. This was exactly what she needed. To feel alive. Happy, healthy and, oh, so alive.

She slid her hands beneath his T-shirt, and he groaned when she tugged at the waistband of his jeans. The clothing was in the way and she wanted it gone.

"Wait—just wait," Jared's chest rose erratically as he gulped air. "I...uh..."

"I don't want to wait." Boldly, Shelly grabbed the hem of her shirt and his eyes nearly torpedoed straight out of his head when she stripped it off. "I want you."

CHAPTER TEN

HER hands were everywhere, searing him with her touch. Pure sensation obliterated rational thought. Shelly was breath-stealing beautiful, from her heart-shaped face to her perfect breasts encased in a pale pink bra and lower to the rounded curve of her stomach.

When she pushed his shirt off his shoulders, Jared couldn't bring himself to stop her. Not when he wanted her more than she could have possibly wanted him.

With amazing boldness, she licked and tasted his chest while her busy fingers fiddled with the button on his jeans. When her fingertips dipped inside, his breath lodged in his throat.

Too fast. Dazed, he tried to gather his scattered brain cells. There was some reason he needed to slow things down, but he was damned if he could remember what it was.

He helped her shuck off his jeans, then peeled hers away as well. With one arm, he pushed aside the few leftover dirty dishes on the kitchen counter. Then, with a swift movement, he lifted her body up onto it.

''Much better.'' Her voice was breathless as they were eye to eye and she sought his mouth with hers.

Her eagerness was his undoing. He made quick work of her bra, filling his hands with her generous, rose-tipped breasts. With a groan he abandoned her mouth and lowered his head to flick his tongue over one engorged nipple.

"Jared. Please… It's been so long. Don't make me wait."

He couldn't deny her anything, and certainly not this. He shucked his boxers and peeled away her filmy pink panties, then paused and turned back to find his jeans. He needed protection, dammit. Did he even have any condoms? His spirits sank. When was the last time he'd even bought any?

"Here, let me." To his amazement, Shelly ripped open a small packet and gently covered him, taking her sweet time, exploring, caressing until he wanted to weep.

"Enough," he growled and pushed her hands away, lest she kill him with pleasure on the spot. The fact that she'd planned for this, prepared for being with him like this, made him burn hotter. Wonderwoman to the rescue again. He did a little exploring of his own.

She was hot, wet and more than ready. With a quick thrust, he sank deep. She gasped and cried out his name, moving urgently against him.

Dozens of lights exploded in his brain and the floor seemingly trembled beneath his feet as the world around them shattered with pleasure. For a long moment he clutched her close, her head cushioned on his chest, her legs wrapped tightly around his hips, while his heart rate slowed, coming down from beyond the danger zone.

Finally, she stirred, lifting her head enough to kiss his neck. Immediately, he felt himself harden inside her.

"My room," she whispered, biting the lobe of his ear.

Yes. He couldn't speak, but gathered his flagging strength and lifted her into his arms. Carelessly, he kicked their discarded clothing out of his way as he headed through the living room and down the hall.

This time, with the rough edge of desire sated, he slowed the pace, taking his time to look at her, burning the image into his memory. He couldn't remember ever feeling like this about anyone. They moved together, slowly, deliberately, as one. Until at last they rose together, soaring to completion.

And fell asleep, tangled in each other's arms, hip to hip, heart to heart.

The insistent ringing of a phone brought Jared reluctantly awake. When he lifted his head, he realized he was alone in the bed. Then his gut clenched in warning when he noticed Shelly standing beside the bed, fully dressed, holding his cell phone in her hand.

"This must be for you," she said, handing him the phone.

Still half-asleep, he took it and pushed the button. "Hello?"

"Jared. Your father and I have been waiting to hear

from you. Have you made arrangements for us to see our grandson?''

He winced at the demanding tone in his mother's voice. Shelly raised a brow and stepped back, giving him the smallest sliver of privacy. ''Uh...no, not yet.''

''What in the world is taking so long?'' His mother was more than a little annoyed. ''You promised us we'd get to see him. I thought for sure you meant this weekend.''

Shelly's back was stiff, and he'd already decided that finding her fully dressed, while he was still naked in her bed, wasn't a good sign. Further, he noticed she'd retrieved their clothes from the kitchen. His jeans and shirt were folded in a nice, neat little pile. How long had it been since he'd struggled through an uncomfortable morning after? Too many months to count.

And he was damned if he planned on having one now.

''This isn't a good time.'' Jared didn't care if his mother was put off by his rudeness. ''I'll call you later.'' He flipped the phone shut and immediately switched it off.

''If you don't mind, I'd like you to go before Tyler wakes up.'' Shelly's voice floated over to him as if she were miles across the most distant sea.

Hell, yes, he minded, but he couldn't risk ticking her off more than she already was. In the early morning light, he studied her profile, silently begging her to look at him.

"Shelly, we need to talk." He inwardly swore, knowing he sounded like a parrot, repeating himself. The time for talking had been last night, but had he done the smart thing? No. Of course not.

She turned her head, a hank of brown hair falling across her cheek. "Please, get dressed. I don't want Ty to see you." With that, she swung away, leaving him alone.

He scrubbed his hands over his face, then reluctantly climbed from her bed and reached for his clothes. This wasn't the way he'd expected to greet the morning but, then again, maybe this way was for the best. He felt sick, knowing just how angry Shelly would be when he told her he knew who she really was.

This was why having relationships wasn't a good idea. He ruined them without even trying.

Walking into the living room, he found Shelly standing at the door. She really intended to kick him out? Without so much as a "Thanks, it's been fun"? Without so much as a kiss goodbye?

"Jared, please, don't." She lifted a hand to stop him from speaking. "What we shared was wonderful, but I can't do this. I can't let Tyler see you here."

"Shelly, he's five. He's not going to understand what happened between us." Annoyance underscored his tone.

"I'll know." Shelly lifted one shoulder negligibly.

''Or he'll make some innocent comment to someone that an adult could hear then they'll know. Please, I'm asking you to go.''

They needed to talk, but clearly this wasn't the time. Not when he could still smell the tangy mixture of sex and the lilac scent of her perfume on his skin. Not when she was so dead set against Ty waking up and finding him here.

He supposed he should be grateful Shelly cared so much for her son. For his nephew. With a sigh, he scratched his jaw, figuring a retreat and regroup might be best.

''I'll see you later, then.'' Jared couldn't bring himself to completely give in to her strong-arm tactics. ''Because we still need to talk. Especially now.''

The light in her eyes dimmed. ''There isn't anything to talk about.''

There certainly was, but she didn't know the half of it. With an abrupt move he yanked her close, planted a searing kiss on her lips, then let go and stepped back before she could regain her senses and slug him one.

''There is. Six o'clock. Dinner. Both you and Ty be ready.'' With that he turned and left.

Outside in his car, he blew out a long breath. The easy part was convincing his parents to give him more time to spring the truth on Shelly. The hard part would be telling Shelly the truth.

Something he should have done before making love with her.

*   *   *

Shelly buried her face in her hands to keep from reaching out to Jared and holding him back as he left. After several long seconds she forced herself to close the door behind him.

This was for the best, she rationalized for the sixth time since she'd woken up early that morning. Making love with Jared had been a mistake. One she'd made with her eyes wide open, fully aware of the line she was crossing. Hadn't she bought the condoms? But it had been a mistake nonetheless.

To keep herself occupied, Shelly returned to the kitchen to clean up the mess she'd used as an excuse last night to avoid reading Ty a story. The lie burned behind her eyes. If Jared had stayed this morning, there'd have been one lie, then another, until soon she wouldn't know where the lies ended and the truth began.

She scrubbed furiously at the counter, trying, without much success, to obliterate the image of how they'd used the surface as a prop in a wild bout of love-making. Dear Lord, what had she been thinking? They'd made love in the kitchen. Ty could have walked in on them, innocently asking for a glass of water. How could she have been so stupid and reckless?

And who was the woman on the phone so early this morning? Shelly hated the nasty kernel of doubt that nibbled its way into her subconscious. She didn't really think Jared had a slew of women on the side. What, really, did she know about Dr Jared O'Connor?

Apart from the fact that he'd recently moved from Boston, was single and had a father suffering from inoperable heart disease?

"Mom, I'm hungry." Tyler broke into her troubled thoughts. She turned to see him standing there, rubbing his sleepy eyes. "What's for breakfast?"

"How about our favorite?" She gave him a quick hug, before he squirmed away.

"Hotcakes and sausage." Ty made a fist and punched the air. "All right."

Shelly tried to keep herself focused on the mundane tasks of laundry and grocery shopping, but whenever she let down her guard, thoughts of Jared would sneak beneath her barriers and zap her with laser-like memories.

That afternoon, she sat in a lawn chair while Ty amused himself with throwing his Nerf football high in the air. She tipped her head back against the aluminum frame of her chair and closed her eyes. What she really needed was a nap. Sleep hadn't been top on her list of priorities last night. Her fault, for thinking with her hormones instead of her brain. Plus, she had to work the 7 p.m. to 7 a.m. shift again tonight.

Tired. She was so darn tired. For several moments she simply floated in a blissful state of relaxation. Maybe she should call Ellen, see if Ty could come over a little earlier so she could get some sleep. Then all she would need was some sort of magic potion to keep Jared from invading her dreams.

Crack! The sound, too much like a rifle shot, had

her bolting up from her chair. Too late, her eyes widened with horror as she watched Tyler fall.

"Mo-om!" His terrified scream split the air and she could have sworn his tiny body bounced as he hit the ground beneath the oak tree with a horrible *thunk*. It took her precious seconds to realize her son had been climbing the tree when the branch had broken.

"Tyler." She fell to her knees at his side. "Oh, God, Tyler. It's OK. Mommy's here." Her hands cradled his head, her gaze raking him for injuries. No blood. Thank heaven. As far as she could see, there was no blood.

"Hurts, it hurts," he sobbed as she struggled to prevent him from moving too much.

"What hurts, Ty?" She gently, very gently log-rolled him onto his back, running a hand down the length of one leg, then the other. Then she saw it, the abnormal bend to his left arm.

"My arm hurts," he cried.

"Don't move." She held him still with a hand planted in the center of his chest. "Stay right here. I'm going to call for help. Don't move, or you'll make it hurt worse."

Satisfied that he would listen, Shelly took precious seconds to sprint into the house and grab the portable phone. She dialed with one hand as she returned to Ty's side.

Feeling slightly better with the ambulance on the way, she bent over her son. From what she could tell, he hadn't suffered any other obvious injures, although there were plenty of potentially invisible ones. Bleeding into his chest, abdomen, head—the list was endless.

She spoke soothingly to her son, a steady stream of mindless chatter, until help arrived.

The paramedics were wonderful, cradling Tyler's broken arm and lifting him carefully into the ambulance. They allowed her to ride along, which she did without hesitation, not caring how she'd manage to get back home.

In the emergency department of Children's Memorial, the hospital staff recognized her and helped get Tyler settled without waiting. At times like this, she was grateful to use whatever leverage her flight nurse status allowed.

The place was busy, the antiseptic scent sharp as the air around her was filled with crying, wailing kids of various ages. They'd gotten into a room, but from there they had to wait their turn.

Shelly closed her eyes and desperately wished she hadn't sent Jared away that morning. Maybe if she had allowed him to stay, this wouldn't have happened. She fought the urge to call him, knowing that this mess was her own fault. Instead, she settled on calling Lifeline. After almost a full year of never calling in sick, she was going to have to take time off again, for the second time in two weeks. On a Saturday night, no less.

She never expected to hear Jared's voice on the other end of the line when she called.

"Jared. This is Shelly. I'm really sorry, but I'm not going to make my shift tonight. I'm in the ED at Children's Memorial with Tyler."

"What happened?" His sharp question pierced her ear.

"He's OK, I think. Fell out of our tree and broke his arm." Shelly was proud of her calm tone. "I am sorry. Calling in at the last minute like this isn't a habit of mine, I swear."

"Don't worry about it. I'll be right there."

To her surprise, he hung up. She frowned as she replaced the receiver. Good grief, hopefully he'd find someone to cover her shift first.

Jared showed up in Tyler's cubicle about fifteen minutes later. He barely glanced at her, just long enough to confirm that Kristin was covering for her, before heading straight for Ty.

"Hey, slugger. How are you?" He placed a hand on her son's shoulder. "Broke your arm, huh?"

"Yeah. I broke it falling out of the tree. My football was stuck. Mom was relaxing in her chair, so I didn't want to bother her."

Shelly's cheeks flushed with guilt. She wouldn't have been relaxing in her chair if she hadn't spent half the night having wild sex with Jared. Why had she bought those stupid condoms?

"They've taken him for X rays, we're just waiting for the results," she offered, avoiding his direct gaze.

"Ms Bennett?" A youthful-looking resident poked

his head through the doorway. "The orthopedic surgeon is here to talk to you."

"Surgeon?" Shelly swallowed hard as a tall, middle-aged man walked into the room.

"I'm Dr Graves." He solemnly shook her hand, then earned points in her book by turning to Ty. "Hello, Ty. Hmm. You sure did a number on your arm, didn't you?"

Her son had stopped crying but there were still wet streaks from his tears staining his cheeks. "Yep. I fell out of the tree and broke it."

"You sure did. Broke it good." Dr Graves turned back to Shelly. "He has a complicated compound fracture of both the radius and ulna. He's going to need surgery, the sooner the better. I can take him in a couple of hours, but I'll need your permission to give him blood."

"Blood?" The room spun as Dr Graves's words registered in her head. "Surgery?"

"Yes. I need you to sign this consent form. There are risks to surgery and I've listed them here. One of the risks is receiving blood, although the blood bank screens everything very carefully—"

"I know the risks," Shelly interrupted him. "I'm a flight nurse for Lifeline."

His expression softened. "We have time, you could donate a unit of blood for him yourself if you'd like."

Tears sprang to her eyes and she blinked rapidly. "I would, but I can't. Tyler's blood type is O-negative. I'm A-positive. I can't donate blood for him." Inwardly she wanted to scream, to rant and rave and shout. This wasn't fair, dammit. Did Ty's grandparents have the same blood type as he did?

"I can donate blood for him." Jared's voice cut through the useless silent rampage in her head.

"What?" She spun toward him. "You can?"

Slowly he nodded. "My blood type is O-negative. Actually…" He walked toward her, grabbed her hands and held them tight as he added in a low tone, "Everyone has O-negative blood in my family. Both my parents, me and my brother, Marc. I know this is a bad time to tell you this, but I know who you are, Shelly. I know your real name is Sharon Leigh Wilson. And I also know Tyler is Marc's son."

CHAPTER ELEVEN

"No." SHE shook her head, not wanting to believe what Jared had just said. She shook her head in an effort to dislodge the giant bumblebee that buzzed in her ears. "I— No. You can't be related."

"It's true. I'm sorry to tell you like this, but I'm not sorry to have found you. We've been looking for you and Ty since you left six years ago."

"Ms Bennett?" The surgeon lost patience with their discussion. "Are you giving consent for your son to have surgery or not?"

"Yes." Grateful, she turned her attention to more important matters—her son. Should she take a chance on using blood from the blood bank for Ty's transfusion? No, she couldn't do it. "If Jared, er, Dr O'Connor will donate blood."

"I'll go over to the blood bank right now," Jared quickly offered.

"Thinking about it, they're not open this late on a Saturday," Dr Graves warned. "You can try the lab, though they don't like to do this sort of thing on a rush basis."

"They'll do it." Jared's tone was firm. "I'll pull whatever strings necessary to make it happen." She couldn't help but believe the silent promise in Jared's eyes as he left.

"Fine, we'll call the OR team." Dr Graves nodded at her and Ty, then followed Jared out of the cubicle.

Alone, Shelly stared at her son. His face was pale against his thick, dark brown hair. And there, in the corners of his eyes, were the tiny crinkles that were so much like his father's.

She'd always known how much her son looked like Marc. She swallowed hard, trying to prevent the sick feeling in her stomach from erupting violently. After all these years, Marc's family had found her. Jared was Marc's brother. He knew her real name.

Jared was Ty's uncle.

Her knees gave away and she collapsed in a nearby chair. Dear God, she hadn't even considered the meaning behind what Jared had told her. They'd searched for her, for Ty. They wanted her son. Just like when they'd tried to buy him from her before he was born, they wanted her son.

"Mom? My arm hurts."

Shelly used every last shred of strength to pull herself together. There would be time to deal with Jared later. Right now, her son needed her. She stood and crossed over to Ty's bedside, then pushed his call button to ring the nurse. "I know, sweetheart. We'll see if they can give you something for the pain, all right?"

"OK." Ty's lower lip trembled. "It hurts really bad. Will the surgery hurt bad, too?"

"Oh, no, honey. The doctor will put you to sleep so you don't feel a thing. After the surgery, your arm might hurt a bit, but you'll get pain medicine then, too. Everything is going to be fine. You'll see.'' Shelly did her best to allay her son's fears.

The nurse brought in another dose of painkiller and injected the medication into Ty's IV. Then the pediatric anesthesiologist came into the room, asking for Ty's health history. He dutifully noted Ty's recent bladder infections and the results of his even more recent tests.

''What about blood?'' the anesthesiologist asked. ''We'll probably need to give him a small blood transfusion during surgery.''

''I know. Jared, er, Dr O'Connor is donating some for him right now.'' She hoped.

''Hmm. OK, we'll make sure we use the donor-directed blood.'' He made another notation, then took out his stethoscope to listen to Ty's heart and lungs. She was impressed with the way he unclipped the small panda hanging from the tubing and showed it to Ty, before putting the cold instrument on his chest. ''This is Paddy the panda. He likes visiting kids like you.''

Ty's face was still scrunched up with pain but he smiled at the small stuffed toy, especially when the doctor clipped the panda onto Ty's finger. ''Hey, I think Paddy likes you.'' He smiled reassuringly at Ty as he quickly listened to his heart tones and lung sounds, then put the stethoscope away. ''You're gonna have a cool cast on your arm. All the kids in your school will get to sign it. Pretty neat, huh?''

Ty's grin was weak, but Shelly could tell he was cheered up at the thought.

Within two hours, the hospital staff had everything ready for Ty's surgery. Jared had succeeded in pulling strings to get his blood donated for Ty and sent immediately to the OR. The two of them walked alongside Ty's gurney as the ED staff wheeled him to the operating rooms. At the door, Shelly leaned down over the gurney to give Ty a hug and a kiss.

"I love you," she whispered against his ear. "You're going to be just fine. I'll be waiting right here for you, I promise."

Ty nodded. "I love you, too."

When Shelly stepped away, Jared took her place. "Hey, Ty, I'll take care of your mom for you while you're gone, OK?"

"Will you be here when I get out?" Ty wanted to know.

"Absolutely. I'll be right here with your mom, waiting for you." She was surprised when Jared leaned down to drop a kiss on the top of Ty's head, his voice thick with emotion as he added, "See you soon."

"See you soon," her son echoed.

Shelly waited until Ty was out of sight behind the OR doors before swiping at her tears and sniffling loudly.

"He'll be fine." Jared wrapped his arm around her shoulders.

For a moment, she leaned on him, not sure her legs would support her otherwise. Poor Ty had looked so brave, she only hoped the operation went off without any complications. All too soon, though, she remembered who Jared was and what he wanted. She regretfully pulled away.

"The waiting room is right around the corner there." She indicated the area with a wave of her hand.

"Let's go." Jared followed her over and sat down in a seat across from hers. "Look, Shelly—"

"Wait." She held up a hand and took a deep breath. "There's just one thing I want you to tell me. How long? Just how long have you known?"

The flash of hesitation in his gaze confirmed her worst fears. The flare of hope in her heart died at his words. "Since Thursday morning, after our Lifeline shift," he quietly admitted.

Two days ago. He'd known her true identity for *days*. Her mind shifted back through time. Since the day before they'd made love.

The nausea in her stomach rose sharply and she struggled with the urge to be sick. She went hot, then cold in the space of a heartbeat. She swallowed hard and prayed for strength. Jared didn't need to know how badly she'd fallen for him.

"Oh, God." She buried her face in her hands. "What is wrong with me? I threw myself at you like some sex-starved widow."

"Shelly, don't. I'm absolutely the luckiest guy in the world to be spending time with you." Jared gently pried her fingers away from her face.

His familiar touch sent shards of longing slicing through her veins. She shook off his hands, stood to widen the distance between them. "Don't touch me.

How could you? Was sleeping with me a part of your master plan? Did you think I'd be more willing to allow you into Ty's life if you had sex with me?''

''Of course not. For heaven's sake, Shelly, I've been attracted to you from the moment I first met you. Don't tell me you didn't feel it, too. Can't you see? What's between us happened long before I knew who you were.''

''I wish I could believe that,'' Shelly murmured, rubbing her hands over her chilled arms. She turned and stared out the window overlooking a cheery courtyard, the rustling leaves changing with the season, turning a bright shade of yellow. The color couldn't ease her torment. ''I didn't even know Marc had a brother until that night. When I told him I was pregnant.''

She sensed Jared coming up to stand behind her and tensed, but he didn't touch her or interrupt.

Closing her eyes, she remembered that fateful night. ''I probably shouldn't have sprung the news on him like I did, but I was upset myself and not thinking clearly. The timing of getting pregnant couldn't have been worse, I only had two more semesters to go until I graduated with my bachelor's degree in nursing.''

''Did you consider the alternative?''

''No!'' Shocked he'd even mention such a thing, she spun around to face him. ''Of course not. And once I got over the shock of it, the constant sickness and exhaustion, I never regretted my decision.''

''So why did you run?'' Jared lightly brushed a stray strand of hair away from her cheek.

"Because of your parents. I— Just trust me on this. I couldn't stay. And you have to promise me that you won't tell you found us." She reached out and grabbed his arms. "Promise me, Jared. I don't want your parents to know where I am."

"Shelly, they already know. They want to meet Ty."

"No! Absolutely not!" Panic snaked up her spine, then wound incessantly around her neck, closing tight. She struggled to suck in a deep breath. "I won't let them see Ty. I won't."

"Calm down, you're not being rational about this." Jared's expression was baffled. "I don't understand. What is wrong with grandparents meeting their grandson? Did they treat you badly, Shelly? Did they refuse to believe your baby was Marc's? What?"

"They tried to buy my baby." With her finger, she stabbed him in the chest, punctuating every word. "Your parents offered me half a million dollars for my son."

Five hundred thousand dollars was a lot of money, so much that Jared had trouble believing what Shelly was telling him. "You must have misunderstood."

The harsh laugh that burst from her chest was anything but mirthful. "No. I didn't misunderstand. Your mother was quite clear on the terms."

Jared didn't know what to say. His mother's reaction to him finding Shelly and Ty had been odd. But he certainly didn't believe they honestly wanted custody of a five-year-old boy. Not when his father's health was tenuous at best.

"Maybe they made a crazy offer out of grief. But you need to know, Shelly, they aren't a threat to you now. No one wants to take Ty away from you."

"I'm sorry, but I can't afford to believe that. Your mother set the terms but your father was the one who threw his legal clout into the bargain. I don't care what you think, my answer is still no. I will not let them see Ty. End of discussion."

Shelly turned and walked to the other side of the room. He let her go. She was clearly upset, between Ty's traumatic injury, needing surgery and finding out he knew about her secret identity. Jared figured she'd reached the point of saturation long ago. No sense in pushing this any further. Ty wasn't in any condition to meet his grandparents right now anyway.

As a matter of fact, Jared figured he'd better call his parents to tell them the news. He'd already had to do some fast talking the other day to keep them from coming out, and to convince his father to have his echocardiogram. Then there was his rude behavior toward his mother when she'd called earlier that morning while he'd been naked and warm in Shelly's bed. Talk about bad timing. Now this latest turn of events.

Jared wandered into the hallway outside the waiting room, and out of Shelly's earshot, to make the call. The phone at his parents' house rang and rang, until the answering machine kicked in.

Jared frowned. Where could they be late on a Saturday afternoon? Had his father been feeling well enough to go out for dinner? He tried his dad's cell phone.

"Hello." The connection wasn't great, but he definitely recognized his father's voice.

"Dad?" Jared hunched his shoulders and turned his back on the waiting room, lowering his voice as much as he dared. "I can barely hear you. Where are you?"

"Glad you called, Jared. We'll be landing soon. You'll need to pick us up at the airport."

"No." He closed his eyes, knowing the answer before he even asked. "Don't tell me you're on the way here to see Ty."

"That's exactly where we are. We're very anxious to meet our grandchild. Our flight is due to arrive at General Mitchell Airport in forty minutes."

Too bad. As far as Jared was concerned, his parents would have to wing it. He'd promised Ty to be there when he got out of surgery, and he was damned if he wouldn't keep his promise. "Sorry, but I can't pick you up. Take a cab and find a hotel. I'll get in touch with you later."

"What do you mean, you can't pick us up? Of course you can. Aren't you the director over at that helicopter place? Surely you can spare a few minutes to pick us up."

He ground his teeth in an effort to hold onto his temper. "That's not the point. You didn't tell me you were coming out today and I refuse to simply rearrange my life for you. Take a cab, find a hotel near the airport. I'll call you later."

Jared hung up before his father could continue to argue. Then he turned his phone off, so they couldn't hound him. With a sigh, he rubbed his jaw. Maybe Shelly had a point about his parents. He was used to their stubbornness but he could see where a young, pregnant woman could easily have been intimidated by them. Hell, he and Marc had often felt the same way. Marc more so, especially after Jared had chosen a career in medicine rather than in following his father's footsteps into law school. Poor Marc had been the one to be sucked into following his father's master plan.

His fault. Everything came back to the fact that Marc's death was his fault. If he hadn't argued, about Shelly no less, Marc would still be alive and Shelly would never have run. If he'd gone into law school, his brother could have chosen a different path. Not that he'd even known how unhappy Marc had been, until the night of his death.

"I'm getting married, Jared. Congratulate me. I'm also going to be a father."

"Married? A father? Are you crazy? You're still in school. How can you afford to get married?"

"I'm dropping out. I never wanted to be a lawyer anyway. In fact, I hate law school. I always have. Why do you think I hang out so much at Stephan's? Well, at least going to Stephan's helped me meet Leigh. And she thinks I should follow my dream of running my own club. That's what I want to do. I don't care what the old man says. Let him cut me out of his will. I don't want his damn money anyway."

"Look, drop out of school if that's what you want. You'll need to work as you'll have a baby to support. But managing a club? And marriage? Hell, Marc, you're insane. Do you even love her?"

"Yeah, I love her, or I wouldn't have proposed. Besides, I refuse to leave Leigh high and dry with a baby to raise. I'm gonna marry her."

"You're crazy. She's a cocktail waitress. There's no reason to marry her. All you need to do is give support for your child. Don't do something stupid," Jared had advised.

"To hell with that. To hell with you! I'm going to quit school and get married. With or without your brotherly support."

Marc had stormed out the door, to crash less than ten miles from his apartment.

Of course, in hindsight, Jared had suspected that some of Marc's comments could have been the alcohol talking, especially since the autopsy had shown Marc's blood alcohol level had been over twice the legal limit. He should have suspected Marc had been drinking, and dropped the whole subject right from the start.

Guilt had been his constant companion ever since that night. Jared knew if Marc were still alive, he'd be the one here right now at the hospital, comforting Shelly. Marc and Shelly would be married, possibly having a second child, this one a girl with her mother's big green eyes. Jealousy nipped at the back of his neck. Was he going nuts? How could he be jealous of his dead brother?

Easy, man. Because Shelly loved Marc. She was intimate with him, created a beautiful child with him. Jared forced himself to admit the truth. He was viciously jealous of the fact Shelly had once loved Marc. Enough to promise to marry him, to bear his child. And knowing Shelly's Wonderwoman tendencies, she would have done everything in her power to make the marriage work. Not like so many others who threw in the towel when they hit the first storm at sea. Wonderwoman wouldn't have let any storm separate her from her man.

Jared turned back toward the waiting area with a deep ache in his heart. He watched as Shelly paced the length of the room. Marc might be dead, but his essence lived on in Jared's guilt. All he could do was make it up to Shelly and Ty somehow.

Starting with mending the rift between Shelly and his parents.

CHAPTER TWELVE

"Ms Bennett?"

Shelly leaped to her feet when a weary-looking Dr Graves entered the room. Jared empathized with the eagerness in her eyes. "Yes?"

"Your son's surgery went fine. I had to put quite a bit of hardware in his arm, so don't be frightened when you see the pins sticking out of his bones."

She visibly gulped. "How many pins?"

"Three in total, here, here and here." Graves demonstrated on his own forearm where he'd placed them. "The contraption looks much worse than it is and I've ordered plenty of pain medication to ensure your son's comfort."

"When can she see him?" Jared asked.

"He'll be sedated for quite a while yet, but I've told the recovery room nurses that you'd insist on coming in. Only for a few minutes, though," he warned. "My patient needs his rest."

"How long do you anticipate keeping him in the hospital?" Jared knew at least overnight, but hoped it wouldn't be much more than that. Shelly already looked bone weary and there was still a long way to go.

"We'll take it day by day but, with Shelly being a

nurse, he should be ready to go home in a couple of days.''

''Thank you, Dr Graves.'' Shelly clasped the doctor's hand fervently with both of hers. ''Thanks for everything.''

He smiled. ''You're welcome. The recovery room is through those doors. They're expecting you.''

Jared followed Shelly in to see Ty. The post-anesthesia recovery unit was a bustle of activity and patients lined three of the four walls. Although he knew what to expect, seeing Ty so tiny and frail against the stark white sheets bothered him. He was so young, and had faced the thought of surgery bravely. Ty opened his eyes in response when Shelly called his name, but the groggy expression on his face told Jared the effects of anesthesia were still strong.

They only stayed a few minutes, then the nurse ushered them out, promising to call when they were ready to send Tyler to his room.

Back in the waiting room, Jared glanced at his watch. Did he have time to meet with his parents to let them know what was going on? He wanted to be there for Ty when he woke up but, by the look of things, that could be several hours from now.

''Shelly, I have a quick errand to run.'' Jared didn't want her to know his parents were in town, she didn't need the added stress on top of everything else. ''I'll be back in an hour.''

''Fine.'' She crossed her arms over her chest, wordlessly announcing she didn't need him anyway. Her attitude had been cool since they'd argued over allowing Ty to meet his parents. Jared wanted nothing more than to turn the clock back to the time she'd welcomed him in her arms, but there was no use wishing for the impossible. He ignored a sharp stab of longing.

"Here's my cell phone number." He jotted it on the back of his card and handed it to her. "Please, call me if they bring him out earlier than expected. I want to be there. I don't want to break my promise to him."

"Then maybe you shouldn't go." Shelly took the card, but didn't agree to call him.

Jared's determination wavered. Was this Shelly's way of asking him to stay? Did he really need to go and see his parents? One more glance at Shelly's closed expression convinced him. Yes, because he absolutely needed to insist that his parents held off on meeting Ty. At least for a few days. Until Shelly had cooled off enough to have a rational conversation. To understand his parents' need to see Ty.

"I'll be back in an hour." He turned and left.

His parents weren't hard to find. Of course, they'd picked the hotel closest to his apartment. He should have figured they wouldn't settle for staying close to the airport, as he'd suggested.

"Ty broke his arm when he fell out of a tree this morning. He underwent surgery, the doctor had to place several pins to keep his bones in place. He's fine," he added quickly, when his parents' faces registered their alarm. "But he's not up to having visitors. Neither, for that matter, is Shelly."

His mother sniffed. "What kind of mother allows her child to climb a tree?"

Jared shot her a narrow look. "Don't go there. Shelly is a wonderful mother. She also holds the key to allowing you to see Ty. Maybe you should try thinking up ways to get on her good side instead of slamming her abilities?"

"Hrmph." His father had more color in his cheeks than Jared had seen in weeks. "We have the law on our side. There's plenty of case law to support our rights as grandparents."

Swallowing a groan, Jared pinched the bridge of his nose between his fingers. This was not going well. He tried another tactic. "Think about what you're saying," he begged. "Shelly and Ty have done fine without you. Without us. Creating animosity, especially by pulling cheap lawyer tactics, isn't going to help."

"Cheap!" His mother leaped to her feet, planting her hands on her hips. "She's the cheap tramp who took off, denying us a chance to see our only grandson."

"And why is that, Mom? What exactly did you say to make Shelly run?" he challenged.

She had the grace to flush. With one hand, she smoothed the wrinkles from her skirt. "I— We were afraid she would do something crazy after finding out Marc was dead. She was a cocktail waitress, for heaven's sake. All we wanted was to give Marc's child a secure future. We didn't mean to scare her off.''

Jared's anger deflated. As much as he wanted to blame his parents for their ridiculous behavior, he knew that none of this would have happened if Marc hadn't died. He should have supported his brother. The fault was solely his own. ''Well, you did. So trust me when I tell you this isn't a good time. Shelly doesn't have an ounce of faith in your intentions and she isn't a cocktail waitress any more. She's a flight nurse. Telling her the law is on your side isn't going to help.''

The stubborn glint in his parents' eyes made him want to groan. ''Don't we all want what's best for Ty?'' Slowly they nodded. ''I know Shelly. Once she understands that meeting you will be good for Ty, I'm sure she'll come round. We need to give her time.''

''Time? Bah, I don't have time,'' his father piped up grumpily, absently rubbing a hand across the center of his chest. ''Who knows when this heart of mine will give out for good?''

''Joe, don't say things like that,'' his mother admonished, stepping over to his side and rubbing a hand down his back.

''Dad, a few days isn't going to hurt.'' Although Jared could understand his father's concern. After waiting six years, a few days would no doubt seem like a lifetime. ''I'll be in touch with you tomorrow. For now, I'm heading back to the hospital.''

"Wait. When tomorrow?" His mother clearly didn't want him to go.

"I don't know, some time tomorrow morning, I guess. I'll call you." He turned and headed back to Shelly and Ty.

On arriving at the hospital, he headed straight to the waiting room where he'd left Shelly. His timing was perfect, they were just wheeling Ty down the hall. Shelly walked beside them, but barely glanced at him.

Ty noticed him, though, and his pinched face lit up. "You're here."

"You bet. And I'm sticking around to see that you get better soon." Jared noticed Ty's left arm was propped up on pillows, three metal pins sticking out of his arm, attached to a stabilizing bar. He ached to ease the boy's pain, but hoped he was helping just by being there.

Once they had Ty settled in his room, Shelly made herself comfortable in the lounge chair next to his bed.

"So, is anything going on at Lifeline?" she asked, keeping her voice low.

"I didn't go to work." He couldn't lie to her, not with everything that had transpired over the past twenty-four hours. He sat across from her, staring down at his clasped hands for a few moments. Slowly he admitted, "I spoke to my parents, to let them know about Ty."

"What, you've been giving them hourly updates? Injury status reports?" Biting sarcasm, even in a furious whisper, didn't suit her. "Have you told them everything? Do they know about his bladder infection, and his kidney tests, too?"

"No. Shelly, don't do this. They care about Ty, too. I needed to explain things because I didn't want them to come out and see him."

"Good, because the answer is still no."

He sighed. She could teach stubbornness to an elephant. "Would you—?"

"No."

He clenched his jaw. Better drop the subject for now. "Is it OK if I stay with you for a while?"

"You can do whatever you want. I don't really care."

Her words cut deep. Jared tried to convince himself she didn't really mean it, but deep down he knew she did. Years of distrust weren't going to disappear overnight. Somehow he needed to find a way to convince her that his parents wouldn't do anything to hurt Tyler.

Or rather, he wouldn't allow his parents to do anything to hurt Tyler. He was on her side. Hers and Ty's. How could he make her believe it?

The night was long, with Ty waking up every couple of hours whimpering in pain. Shelly jumped up instantly the moment he stirred, attentive to his every need. She even took to assisting with Ty's pain medication, staying at his side, cradling him and murmuring words of comfort until the medication took hold.

His parents were wrong. Ty couldn't have a better mother than Shelly, Jared thought.

His presence was extraneous. He sat in the corner of Ty's room, watching Shelly, mesmerized by her intensity in caring for her son. She didn't need him, she had everything under control. He had no doubt that she would easily get through the next few days, until Ty was truly on the mend.

Shelly would never know how he secretly remembered the one night when her intensity had been focused on him, on the pleasure they'd had together. He longed to go back to that time, but deep down he was forced to acknowledge that time was over. Shelly wouldn't invite him back now. But no matter what happened, he would gratefully remember, for the rest of his life, every minute they'd spent together.

By the time the doctor came around, Jared knew it was time for him to go. Although Shelly wasn't as cool to him as she'd been the night before, he was conscious of the fact that Ty had no idea they were related. Shelly wasn't about to tell Ty he had an uncle.

And nothing was going to change the fact that he wasn't Ty's father. He couldn't live Marc's life.

Jared was just getting ready to leave when the door to Ty's room unexpectedly swung open. His jaw nearly hit the floor when he saw his parents standing there.

"Hello, Ty." His mother boldly entered the room first, carrying an oversize soft toy in her arms. But his father wasn't far behind. Beside him, he heard Shelly suck in a harsh breath.

"Hi." Ty's head swung toward them, his eyes widening with childlike interest when he spied the toy. "Who are you?"

Jared's mother beamed, her eyes suspiciously moist, completely oblivious to the emerald daggers Shelly shot at her from the opposite side of Ty's bed. "We're your grandparents, Ty. Your daddy was our son. We're your Grandma and Grandpa O'Connor."

CHAPTER THIRTEEN

GET out! Shelly silently screamed, her knuckles white as she gripped Ty's side rail. *Get out and leave my son alone!*

But the words stuck in her throat. Helpless to stop what was happening, she glared at Jared. How could he have betrayed her wishes? Had he planned this little visit all along? Was this why he'd asked to stay, not for Ty's benefit or even hers, as she'd hoped, but rather for his own personal agenda? How could she have misjudged him so badly?

"Is that for me?" Ty's hopeful gaze had locked on the giant soft toy in the woman's arms.

"It certainly is." Elizabeth O'Connor bravely approached Ty's bed.

Already, she thought, the O'Connors were trying to use their wealth to win Ty. No way would she allow them to succeed.

"I'm sorry, but Ty isn't really up for visitors." Shelly finally found her voice, doing everything in her power to remain polite when her instincts were shrieking at her to grab Ty and run.

"We won't stay long." Joseph O'Connor stepped forward, forming a united front with his wife, silently challenging Shelly to physically toss them out. "After all this time, a few moments shouldn't matter."

She narrowed her gaze, tightening her grip on the rail. Throwing Marc's parents out would be sweet, but Ty was too young to witness such violence. Especially from his mother.

"Are you really my grandma and grandpa?" Ty asked, his gaze swinging between the two of them.

"Yes, we really are." Elizabeth's expression softened as she turned toward Ty, and Shelly nearly whimpered in distress. No, this couldn't be happening. Ty belonged to her, he was her son. Why didn't Marc's parents just go back to Boston where they belonged?

"Cool." Ty's eyelids drooped, but he fought sleepiness, forcing them back open. "'Cause it's Grandparents' Day at school next week and I didn't want a pretend one."

"A pretend one?" Elizabeth echoed with a frown, leaning closer.

"You know, there are some grandmas and grandpas that don't have grandkids of their own, so they come and pretend to be ours." His eyelids drooped again, and his words slurred. "But I'm glad t'have my own…" He succumbed to the effects of the pain medication.

Shelly's shoulders slumped, her anger deflating. She hadn't known anything about Grandparents' Day. Ty hadn't said a word about the event until now.

"We'll be there, Ty, I promise." Elizabeth's voice broke and she turned toward her husband who put a reassuring arm around her shoulders. "Did you hear that Joseph? Grandparents' Day…"

"As you can see, Ty is exhausted. He needs to rest." Shelly kept her voice firm, her eyes daring them to push. "Please, leave."

"Mom, Dad, come with me." Jared stood, his expression grim. "I'll take you back to the hotel."

"Oh, but—"

"*Now.*" Jared's voice was firm, as he overrode his mother's protest. "You've seen Ty for yourself. Maybe you can come back later."

Over my dead body, Shelly thought, but she watched as Joseph and Elizabeth tore themselves away with obvious reluctance, following Jared to the door. Jared's jaw was clenched, his blue eyes dark with repressed fury. He was angry? With her? What on earth had he expected—that she'd welcome his parents with open arms? That she'd forgive his ultimate betrayal?

Not a chance. When they'd left her alone, she sank into the chair and buried her face in her hands, fighting tears. Dear God, what could she do now? Running away and hiding had worked once. Maybe she'd go all the way to the West Coast this time, but how long until they found her again? If she wanted to work as a nurse, her license would leave a paper trail a mile wide for anyone to follow.

No, she couldn't uproot Ty from his friends and drag him halfway across the continent. It was time she faced her past. Shelly lifted her head, her gaze falling on the oversize stuffed toy grinning at her from Ty's bed.

Ty wanted grandparents, and not, she suspected,

only because of Grandparents' Day at school. How could she deny his desire for a normal family? Not only did he have suddenly have doting grandparents, but he also had Uncle Jared. Jared, who had wormed his way into their life. Who had made love to her as if she were the most desirable woman on the planet. Who had traveled over a thousand miles just to find Ty, and in the process had broken her heart with his lies.

Tears leaked down her cheeks. She'd have been better off alone.

Shelly couldn't believe Jared had the nerve to come back an hour after he'd escorted his parents back to their hotel. He caught her as she was leaving Ty's room to take a break while he was asleep.

"I'm sorry" was his greeting on meeting her outside Ty's room.

"Don't even try to tell me that wasn't planned." Shelly wasn't in the mood to hear any more of his lies. Hadn't there been enough already?

He nodded and held up his hands. "You want to believe that, fine. I can't say I'm completely sorry it happened this way. Now you can see for yourself that my parents don't mean any harm. They just want to see their grandson."

"They want to buy him, you mean." Shelly couldn't prevent the bitterness in her tone as she turned and headed down the hall. "Just like they tried to buy him before he was born."

"Shelly, wait." He grabbed her arm, but she

quickly shook him off. "Don't let this animosity ruin what we have. Let's talk about this—please?"

"About what?" Furious, she rounded on him. "About how you lied to me? How you did the one thing I asked you not to do? You used me to get to Ty."

"Don't be ridiculous." Jared stared at her. "I already told you, I fell for you long before I knew who you were."

"And I fell for you before I knew you were scum," she countered. "You and your parents want to see Ty? Fine. I'll agree to a few visits. But as far as not ruining what we have? That's impossible because we don't have anything."

"You don't mean that." The anguish in his gaze tugged at her.

"Yes, I do." Shelly steeled her resolve. "There is nothing between us, Jared. And there never will be."

She turned and continued her way to the elevator at the end of the hall. Without glancing back, she knew Jared hadn't followed her. He still stood where she'd left him in the middle of the hall. She told herself she was glad—he'd finally got the message.

As she traveled down the elevator to the floor housing the cafeteria, she told herself she didn't need him. She didn't need anyone. She was just fine by herself. This mess with Marc's parents only proved that. She'd have been better off if she'd never met Jared in the first place.

But the hollow knowledge formed a pit in her stomach, completely ruining her appetite.

* * *

Alone on the following Monday evening, Jared sat in his office, contemplating the bottle of Scotch he'd bought on the way over. The Lifeline crew was out on a flight, but the peace and quiet in the hangar didn't ease the torment in his heart.

Was this how desperate Marc had felt when he'd taken to going to Stephan's night after night, starting with one drink then having another, and another until he just hadn't cared any more? Looking back, he should have realized Marc had been developing a drinking pattern, but he had been too wrapped up in his own career to give much thought to his brother.

Until it had been too late.

He held the palms of his hands over his burning eyes. All the lives he'd saved as a physician, the way he'd found Shelly and Ty for his parents—nothing he had done could erase his guilt over Marc's death. Why had he thought otherwise? Why should Shelly forgive him, when he knew she was right? He didn't deserve her caring, not when his actions had stolen Marc from her and Ty for ever.

The bottle of Scotch, the promise of oblivion, beckoned to him. He paused in the act of reaching for it when there was a knock at his door.

With a frown, he dropped his hand and called out, "Come in."

He couldn't have been more surprised when Shelly opened the door and walked in. She didn't smile when she asked, "Do you have the schedule?"

"Huh?" Jared stared at her in stunned surprise.

"You know, the flight schedule. I called earlier, but they said you were working on it. I need to figure out when I can work."

So she wasn't handing in her resignation, at least not yet. Jared glanced blankly at his desk, then noticed the corner of the schedule buried beneath a stack of paper. He pulled it out and handed it to her. "You can take all the time you need," he gruffly told her. "I'm sure we'll manage to cover your shifts."

"I can't afford to be off any longer," Shelly informed him, staring with apparent fascination at the schedule in her hands. "My hot-water heater went kaput. Ellen, my sitter, is with Ty right now and, according to Dr Graves, he'll be discharged first thing in the morning. I think I can pick up some shifts starting on Wednesday, even though Ty won't go back to school for another week or so. Ellen has agreed to watch him."

She was avoiding his gaze, and Jared racked his brains to think of something to say. He'd happily buy her another hot-water heater if that's what was causing the financial crunch, but he knew she'd slap that offer back in his face. He almost told her his parents would love to stay with Ty while she worked, but bit his tongue before the words could spill forth. Shelly would rather mud-wrestle ten gorillas than allow him or his parents any influence over her son.

"How is he doing?" Jared forced the question past his constricted throat.

"Better. His arm still hurts but he's already managed to do a fair number of tasks one-handed." She reached over and took a pen from Jared's desk, then proceeded to write her name in the schedule. "I see Kristin was supposed to be off on Wednesday and Thursday. I'll work those shifts for her."

"I'll let her know." The conversation was stilted, uncomfortably so. But he couldn't figure out a way to ease it. Once they had communicated on another level entirely.

But those days were gone.

Shelly set the schedule down, then glanced pointedly at the bottle sitting on his desk. "Are you planning to drink that?"

"No." He knew he wouldn't drink it, but would keep it as a reminder of how he'd failed Marc. "Although I was tempted, until I realized a bottle of Scotch wasn't going to ease my guilt. If finding you and Ty didn't work, nothing will."

Her brows pulled together in a frown. "Guilt?"

He hesitated, then figured she may as well know it all. "Yeah, guilt. Over causing Marc's death. He came to me that night after you told him you were pregnant. I should have known he'd been drinking. He told me he was going to quit school and marry you."

"He did?" She sounded surprised.

"We argued. I tried to talk him out of it."

"Why? He hated law school," Shelly interrupted.

"Not that, I tried to talk him out of marrying you." Jared lifted his gaze to hers. "Do you understand? I told him he was crazy, that he didn't know what he was doing. I never should have tried to talk him out of marrying you. But I did, and we argued, and ten minutes later he was dead.''

"Oh, no,'' she whispered, covering her mouth with her hand. "I had no idea.''

"So, you see, finding you and Ty was the least I could do, to make up for Marc's death. I don't expect your forgiveness. Hell, I can't forgive myself. I don't know why I thought I could replace Marc in Ty's life. I suck at relationships, I always have. I'll never be able to replace Ty's father. Only the man you fall in love with, the man you eventually marry, has that right.'' The truth, spoken so boldly, tore at his heart. He'd fallen in love with Shelly, but he also knew he was the last man on earth she would ever love in return. "If I hadn't interfered, you and Marc would be happily married by now.''

Shelly didn't speak, didn't say a word. She simply stared at him for a long moment, then spun on her heel and ran.

The bottle of Scotch loomed more and more temptingly as Jared sat alone in his office once again.

Shelly didn't stop running until she was outside, in Lifeline's parking lot. Her breath heaved from her lungs as she searched for her car.

A cramp in her side had her doubling over, gasping with pain. Why was she running? You couldn't run from your memories, she'd learned that the hard way.

You and Marc would be happily married by now. Jared's words echoed over and over in her head. They weren't true, but she couldn't tell him that now.

Couldn't make herself tell him she would never have married Marc.

She shook her head, dislodging the haunting memories. She didn't have time for this. To stand here thinking about Marc, about Jared. About the real reason Jared had tracked her down. She didn't want to empathize with him or understand him.

She certainly didn't want to know how badly Jared had longed to be a father to Ty.

Where was she parked? There. She saw her car, ran over to it, then quickly climbed behind the wheel. She drove to Children's Memorial, trying to calm herself before making her way back to Ty's room. Her hands were shaking when she opened the door and pasted a bright smile on her face.

"Did you get your schedule worked out?" Ellen wanted to know.

She nodded. "Wednesday and Thursday, if that's OK with you."

"Perfectly fine. I'm sure Alex will appreciate having his friend back." Ellen smiled as she motioned for her son to get off Ty's bed. "Come on, Alex, we need to go."

"Aw, Mom, why?" Alex acted as if he'd been separated from Ty for months instead of a few days.

"Because I said so." Ellen rolled her eyes at Shelly. "Emma's probably ripping Daddy's hair out as we speak."

A smile tugged at the corner of Shelly's mouth as she pictured Ellen's husband Jeff playing dolls with little Emma. She could easily imagine Jared doing the same thing.

Stop it, she told herself sternly. Jared could have his own children some day, he didn't need Ty.

And he certainly didn't need her.

She walked Ellen and Alex to the door, giving Ellen a quick hug of thanks before she left. She was watching them leave when a familiar-looking woman approached.

Jared's mother. She quickly closed Ty's door, standing before it like a sentinel guarding the gate.

"Hello, Shelly." Elizabeth didn't seem the least bit daunted by Shelly's almost military presence. "I'm glad to see you're here. I wanted to talk to you, alone."

Shelly lifted her chin. "I don't think we have anything to discuss."

"That's where you're wrong." Elizabeth's smile faded. "I know I did you a grave injustice six years ago and I'd like to make amends. I think it's time I got to know a little more about the woman my son loved enough to want to marry."

CHAPTER FOURTEEN

THE sick feeling in Shelly's stomach quadrupled in force. Obviously, Marc's mother didn't know the truth either. No one did. Shelly absolutely didn't want to be the one to enlighten her.

"Honestly, this isn't necessary." Shelly struggled for composure.

"I think it is." Elizabeth glanced up and down the hospital corridor. "We can talk here or go someplace quiet—it's up to you."

Shelly hesitated, then gave in. "Give me a minute to let Ty know I'll be gone."

She ducked her head inside Ty's room, to find him engrossed in a Disney movie on the television. Perfect. "Ty, I need to take a walk for a few minutes. Will you be all right alone?"

"Sure." He hugged his toy close, barely sparing her a glance.

"Great. See you soon."

Back in the hall, Marc's mother waited patiently. Shelly led the way to the small visitors' lounge at the end of the hall.

"Mrs O'Connor—" Shelly began.

"Oh, please, call me Elizabeth." For the first time Shelly noticed the older woman nervously twisting her wedding ring on her finger. "Heavens, you were practically my daughter-in-law."

Oh, boy. Shelly rubbed her damp palms on her jeans. This was going to be worse than she'd thought.

"Besides, I need to apologize for my behavior that night." Elizabeth's voice wavered. "Try to understand, I was out of my mind with grief when you arrived. To lose a child…" She swallowed hard, then continued, "I only pray you never have to experience what I did that night."

Shelly glanced down at her hands, knowing exactly what Marc's mother was talking about. Fear of losing your son was nothing compared to the pain of living through it. If anything happened to Ty—she couldn't complete the thought. As horrible as that night had been, Shelly suddenly understood the older woman's underlying motivation.

"I hope so, too," she murmured.

"There, now, stop it or we'll both be sobbing." Elizabeth took out a crumpled tissue, dabbed at her eyes then blew her nose daintily.

Shelly couldn't help but smile as she swiped her hands beneath her eyes. "I know what you mean. I don't think I ever cried until I had Tyler."

"Exactly. Kids have a way of doing that to you, even when they're older." Elizabeth sighed in relief. "Anyway, I want to welcome you and Ty into our family."

Shelly's smile faded. "You're being very nice, Mrs O'Connor, I mean Elizabeth, but I think there's something you should know." She paused, then forced herself to tell her the truth. "Marc did propose to me the night he found out I was pregnant. But I never promised to marry him. I actually didn't answer at all. I was so overwhelmed with the idea of having a baby before I'd manage to graduate that I couldn't really comprehend Marc's proposal." Shelly forced herself to meet Elizabeth's gaze.

"That's OK, dear." Elizabeth patted her hand soothingly. "I understand."

Shelly shook her head, then said in a rush, "No, I don't think you do. I cared about Marc, very much. But we'd jumped into the physical part of our relationship too quickly, and soon I knew we were better off as friends. He assumed my silence was agreement but, in fact, I knew I couldn't do it. I couldn't marry Marc, you see, because…I didn't love him."

She knew Marc had been at Stephan's that night—hadn't he always been? And, of course, he'd had a few drinks. She shouldn't have sprung the news of her pregnancy on him like that, but she'd needed someone to talk to. When Marc had proposed, she hadn't been able to bring herself to answer. He hadn't pushed, but had quickly left, saying something about getting things lined up for their future. Had Marc seen the truth in her eyes? She thought so, but she'd never know for certain.

Jared blamed himself for Marc's death, but Shelly knew with deep certainty that the fault was equally hers.

*   *   *

Late on Wednesday night, Jared entered the Lifeline lounge to find Shelly seated on the sofa, her head tipped back, her eyes closed. She looked pale and drawn, obviously exhausted, but achingly lovely.

Just like the moment he'd first seen her.

He longed to gather her close, smooth away the lines of fatigue with a kiss. But she wasn't his to hold. Seeing her like this, close enough to touch, Jared wondered if he should tender his resignation after all. Not seeing Shelly would be less torturous than working with her on a daily basis, knowing exactly what he was missing.

He shouldn't have offered to switch shifts with Evans, but the guy wanted more time with his wife and newborn baby and Jared couldn't blame him. Hell, if he had a family...

But he didn't. All the more reason to help out those who did.

As if sensing his presence, Shelly's eyes flew open and met his gaze. Guilty of gawking again, Jared mentally cursed.

"Jared." She sat up on the sofa, blinking in confusion. "What time is it?"

"Just after midnight." He knew how disoriented she felt. Working swing shifts could really mess with your brain. "Don't worry, you didn't sleep through the shift. It's been a quiet night." Their pagers shrilled in unison. "Or was, until I opened my big mouth," he muttered.

"'Motor vehicle crash involving teenagers,'" Shelly read her message out loud. She glanced up at

Jared with a frown. "Requesting adult and pediatric response. Sounds bad."

"Let's go."

Reese had the chopper revved up and ready to fly in less than two minutes. They were airborne in less than five. A hard knot formed in Jared's belly as they banked and headed for the scene. Motor vehicle crashes, especially at night, always reminded him of Marc.

The scene was bad, though no worse than he'd expected. They were immediately flagged toward one car, or what appeared to be half a car. The other half was crumpled beyond recognition.

"We just managed to get the two teens out after a lengthy extrication. The sixteen-year-old boy was driving, but the girl is younger. Has a high school ID but no temporary license."

He and Shelly split up, Jared instinctively taking the older boy. The paramedic had just started CPR. He felt for a pulse. "Good pulse with CPR."

"Do you want me to hold off for a minute?" The paramedic asked when he reached the end of his cycle.

Jared nodded his agreement. The boy's pulse immediately vanished. "No pulse, continue CPR."

"I think he's bleeding into his head, bad." The paramedic commented during a pause in which they checked for the spontaneous return of his rhythm. "Both pupils are blown."

Damn. Jared knew, with sinking certainty, that the kid wasn't going to make it. "Hyperventilate him, if we can at least get his heart to respond, he'll have a chance.''

But they couldn't get his heart to respond, and after nearly an hour of trying Jared agreed to give up. For a long moment he and the paramedics stared down at the dead boy.

Such a waste. Sixteen was too young to die. But all the emergency medicine knowledge in the world couldn't save everyone. His own expertise, such as it was, couldn't bring life back to this one sixteen-year-old kid. Briefly closing his eyes, he tried to shake off the desolation before turning and crossing over to where Shelly knelt beside her patient.

''Come on, dammit, come on.'' She was delivering electric shocks to the girl, with what appeared to be a transient return to her rhythm. ''Stay with me.''

He dropped to his knees on the other side of her. ''Give me an intra-cardiac needle, I think she has tamponade.''

''I did try to tap her once. Maybe you'll have better luck,'' Shelly muttered between compressions.

Jared wasn't so sure he possessed anything close to luck, but gave it his best shot. At first he didn't get anything, then he changed the angle and hit pay dirt. The syringe filled with blood.

''Yes!'' Shelly cried. ''That's it.''

The girl's cardiac rhythm stabilized. With one meaningful glance, they wordlessly agreed to transport her immediately. ''Trinity Medical Center,'' Jared told her. He estimated the girl was barely fifteen, but by the condition of her heart he suspected her needs would be better met at Trinity and the adult cardiothoracic surgeons there.

Reese had the helicopter ready to go. He and Shelly quickly loaded the girl into it, then climbed aboard. Twice Jared pulled more blood from around her heart during the flight, so much so that he requested an open-heart surgeon meet them in the ED.

"What's the problem?" the surgeon asked.

"Repeated cardiac tamponade. I think she has a bleeder you'll need to fix in the OR."

"Are her parents able to give consent?"

Jared shrugged. "I don't think she has much time. I'd take her now."

The surgeon didn't argue, but whisked the patient away. Jared and Shelly stood for a moment in the ED, answering questions about the second victim in the car.

"He didn't make it," Jared confessed.

"Brittany! Where's my daughter?"

Jared turned to see a hysterical woman being held by two nurses. He and Shelly rushed over to help.

"My daughter was in a car accident. Where is she? I want to see her." The woman's voice rose in alarm.

"She's in surgery. They're trying to fix her heart." Shelly's even tone seemed to penetrate the woman's hysteria.

"Did you see her? Is she going to live?"

"I saw her. We kept her alive long enough to get her to surgery." Shelly's voice was calm, soothing. "You're going to have to calm down and give the doctors a chance."

"Oh, God." The woman crumpled before their eyes. "We had a fight. She snuck out of her room. My last words to her were in anger. What if I never get the chance to tell her I love her?" The woman sobbed while Shelly hung onto her shoulders and led her to the nearest chair.

Jared watched as Shelly managed to reassure the woman, that she'd have a second chance with her daughter, even though he wasn't so sure Shelly was telling her the truth. He knew better than anyone there weren't always second chances.

He hadn't been given one with Marc.

While Shelly finished consoling Brittany's mother, Jared called the paramedic base to let them know that the transport was finished, although they were still going to be tied up for a few minutes. It was close to three in the morning—only four more hours to go until the end of the shift. The base radioed Reese, who decided to take the opportunity to refuel. Jared agreed to meet Reese on the helipad in a half-hour.

Thank God for the ED nurses, he found fresh coffee in their lounge. Shelly followed him a few minutes later. "Smells like heaven."

"Hits the spot, too." He eyed her over the rim of his mug. "Is Brittany's mom going to be all right?"

Shelly's smile slid sideways. "If her daughter survives the surgery. Otherwise, I'm not so sure."

Jared nodded. "I know. I don't think you should have given her any possible false hope."

Shelly frowned and carefully set her cup down. "What do you mean?"

"There aren't any second chances. I argued with Marc and he died. There isn't anything I can do to change that."

She stared at him. "What if I told you it was my fault? Would you forgive me?"

Of course he would, but that wasn't the point. "Shelly, trust me, it wasn't your fault."

"I didn't love him," she blurted out. "He asked me to marry him and I didn't answer because I knew I couldn't. I didn't love him. And I think, deep down, he saw the truth in my eyes."

Jared frowned. That wasn't the way he remembered it. "Marc was certain the two of you were getting married. In fact, I distinctly remember asking him if he loved you and he said yes."

She winced and glanced away. "He thought he did, but he was just being nice. The baby was the excuse he needed to quit school. We wouldn't have got married. So, you see, his death is as much my fault as yours. If you can forgive me, you'll have to forgive yourself." Shelly stepped closer, taking the half-empty cup from his hand and setting it aside so she could take his hands in hers.

He marveled at her hands. Her grip was firm, infused with the strength of Wonderwoman.

"I think, after tonight, I believe in second chances, Jared." Shelly's voice was soft. "Think about what that woman said, about parting in anger. Life is too short to hold a grudge. Isn't that what carrying guilt amounts to? If the situation were reversed, you'd forgive me. So what is it really that you're blaming Marc for?''

For dying. The realization hit hard. Dammit, he blamed Marc for dying. For drinking and driving. For putting their family through such grief.

For leaving Shelly to raise Ty alone.

''I...don't blame Marc.'' The words sounded uncertain to his own ears. ''I should have supported him.''

''And he should have been responsible enough not to drink and drive.'' Shelly voiced the thoughts that whirled in his head. ''I cared about Marc, but that doesn't mean he was perfect. None of us are. So if it's OK for Marc to do some things wrong, then it's OK for us, too.''

How was it that she made sense of chaos? Suddenly, everything seemed crystal clear. ''You're right.'' Jared tugged on her hands, pulling her close. She wrapped her arms around him, and he inhaled deeply, filling his head with her lilac scent. ''Life *is* too short to hold a grudge. I've seen enough death to know that. Guilt blinded me so I couldn't see the truth.''

''Me neither.'' Shelly drew partially away, meeting his gaze. ''I was wrong to get angry with you, Jared. I treated you badly. I never told you how thankful I am for your kindness in donating your blood for Ty's surgery.''

''I'm the one who should apologize.'' Jared lifted his hand to smooth a strand of hair away from her face. "Donating blood was nothing, I'd do anything for you. For Ty." He hesitated. *Tell her,* the tiny voice in the back of his head shouted. *Tell her how much you love her, you idiot. Don't chicken out now.*

"Oh, Jared." His heart sank when her eyes misted. Was this the same expression she'd given Marc? Was she telling him right now that she could never love him?

Before he could try to explain how he felt, his pager went off. As much as he was tempted to toss the blasted thing across the room, Shelly pulled away from him, reaching for hers as well.

"Reese has finished refueling." Shelly frowned. "I didn't know he'd gone."

"Yeah. Well, I told him we'd meet on the helipad." Damn Reese for his lousy timing.

"Of course." Shelly blinked, as if trying to remember the way. "We better go meet him. What time is it anyway?"

"Time I told you the truth." Jared grabbed her hands before she could completely slip away. This wasn't the most romantic place on earth, but he couldn't let this moment pass. "I love you, Shelly. I fell in love with you the moment I saw you dancing around your house, blowing that silly horn and wearing that goofy hat, celebrating Ty's health. I know you're strong and independent. I know you don't really need anyone, but I need you. Will you, please, marry me?"

Shelly stared at him for a long minute. The hopeful light in his eyes dimmed and she realized he was taking her silence for no. She clutched his hands and squeezed them tight. "Jared, I do need you. You have no idea how much. These past few days have been pure hell without you. You think I'm strong? What a laugh. I'm not."

"You worked two part-time jobs to get yourself through college, had a child without any help, financial or otherwise, moved to a strange town and managed to become a flight nurse." Jared raised his brows. "I'm feeling like medical school is insignificant compared to all that."

She rolled her eyes but couldn't help but laugh. "Hardly. But you didn't let me finish. I love you, too. I realized just how much that same night, when you readily joined my impromptu celebration."

"Thank God, Shelly." He buried his face in her hair and she smiled, leaning against his chest. "You had me worried there for a minute."

Their pagers went off again. Shelly let out a long sigh. "Reese is obviously getting impatient. I guess we'd better go."

"Yeah. In less than four hours, our shift will be over." Jared's eyes darkened. "Will you let me come home with you?"

"Yes." Her simple answer made him grin.

She didn't complain when Jared kept his arm around her waist as they left the nurses' lounge. On the elevator ride to the top of the building, Jared glanced down at her.

"Do you think Ty will mind when we tell him the news?"

"No." Shelly's expression softened. "He's always wanted a father. And he couldn't have a better one than you."

Before the elevator doors opened, he pulled her close and kissed her. Not just a hard kiss, but one filled with pent-up desire and longing, one that held a silent promise of more. When the doors opened, he broke off the kiss and whispered, "Without you, I'd never have believed in second chances."

Reese stood outside on the helipad beside his chopper, standing close to the building to shelter from the wind. His gaze narrowed on them with annoyance. "What in the blazes took you guys so long? I'm freezing my butt up here."

Shelly walked over and leaned up to press a kiss to his cheek. "Don't be angry, Reese. Congratulate us. Jared and I are getting married."

"Hot damn." Reese's anger faded and he clapped a hand on Jared's shoulder, shaking his head at the radiant expression on Shelly's face. "I think I just won twenty-five bucks in the dating pool."

0205/03a

MILLS & BOON®

Live the emotion

HIS LONGED-FOR BABY by Josie Metcalfe

(The ffrench Doctors)

On the eve of her marriage Dr Maggie ffrench's lifelong dream is shattered – the wedding is cancelled! In the emotional aftermath she finds herself making passionate love to her boss, Jake Lascelles. Now Maggie is pregnant with his child – and she doesn't know why Jake won't believe her...

EMERGENCY: A MARRIAGE WORTH KEEPING
by Carol Marinelli *(A&E Drama)*

Spanish consultant Salvador Ramirez and nurse Isla Ramirez had a happy, passionate marriage. But when their little son died in a car accident Salvador found it impossible to face anyone who reminded him of his child – including his wife. But at work he and Isla are pushed together, and slowly he realises they still need each other...

THE GREEK DOCTOR'S RESCUE by Meredith Webber

(Mediterranean Doctors)

Dr Nik Conias dedicates his life – and his family millions – to his aid organisation, KidCare. It's all he cares about – until he meets nurse Ellie Reardon. Ellie has vowed never to love again, but Nik's charm and caring make him impossible to resist. They're saving lives side by side – but can they help themselves find a future...?

On sale 4th March 2005

Available at most branches of WHSmith, Tesco, ASDA, Martins, Borders, Eason, Sainsbury's and all good paperback bookshops.

Visit www.millsandboon.co.uk

MILLS & BOON®

0205/03b

Live the emotion

Medical
romance™

THE DOCTOR'S PREGNANCY SURPRISE by Kate Hardy

(London City General)

Dr Holly Jones has never recovered from the shock of
losing David Neave's baby — nor from the way he
disappeared from her life. Years later they find
themselves working together in A&E, and as their long-
held secrets come bubbling to the surface they begin to
renew their very special bond. Until Holly discovers
she's pregnant again!

THE CONSULTANT'S SECRET SON by Joanna Neil

Dr Allie Russell is managing the best she can — juggling
her work in A&E and Search & Rescue with her two-
year-old son. Then Nathan Brewster arrives back in her
life as the new A&E consultant. He doesn't know he's
Matty's father, and Allie wants to keep it that way. But
as she and Nathan draw closer again, it's only a matter
of time before he discovers the truth!

NURSE IN RECOVERY by Dianne Drake

Charge nurse Anna Wells's life has been shattered by
an accident. She needs someone very dedicated and
special to help her put the pieces back together...
someone like brilliant Rehabilitation doctor Mitch
Durant. But Mitch is burnt out, the last thing he needs
is another patient — until he sees Anna and realises
she's a challenge he just has to take on...

On sale 4th March 2005

*Available at most branches of WHSmith, Tesco, ASDA, Martins,
Borders, Eason, Sainsbury's and all good paperback bookshops.*

Visit www.millsandboon.co.uk

0305/024/MB120

MILLS & BOON

A *very special*

Mother's

Day

Margaret Way
Anne Herries

Indulge all of your romantic
senses with these two
brand-new stories..

On sale 18th February 2005

Available at most branches of WHSmith, Tesco, ASDA, Martins, Borders,
Eason, Sainsbury's and all good paperback bookshops.

CODE RED

ORDINARY PEOPLE
EXTRAORDINARY CIRCUMSTANCES

PROTECTING
HER MEANS
PUTTING HIS
LIFE ON THE
LINE

Lawyer Faith Lawton steps outside the courthouse.
Shots ring out. The concrete around Faith
explodes with expended bullets as a pair of strong
arms pull her back into the building...

Available from 4th March

Available at most branches of WH Smith, Tesco, ASDA, Martins, Borders,
Eason, Sainsbury's and all good paperback bookshops.

CODE RED/RTL/2

FREE

4 BOOKS AND A SURPRISE GIFT!

We would like to take this opportunity to thank you for reading this Mills & Boon® book by offering you the chance to take FOUR more specially selected titles from the Medical Romance™ series absolutely FREE! We're also making this offer to introduce you to the benefits of the Reader Service™—

★ **FREE home delivery**
★ **FREE gifts and competitions**
★ **FREE monthly Newsletter**
★ **Books available before they're in the shops**
★ **Exclusive Reader Service offers**

Accepting these FREE books and gift places you under no obligation to buy; you may cancel at any time, even after receiving your free shipment. Simply complete your details below and return the entire page to the address below. You don't even need a stamp!

YES! Please send me 4 free Medical Romance books and a surprise gift. I understand that unless you hear from me, I will receive 6 superb new titles every month for just £2.69 each, postage and packing free. I am under no obligation to purchase any books and may cancel my subscription at any time. The free books and gift will be mine to keep in any case.

M5ZEE

Ms/Mrs/Miss/Mr...Initials ....
BLOCK CAPITALS PLEASE

Surname ....

Address ....

....

....Postcode ....

Send this whole page to:

The Reader Service, FREEPOST CN81, Croydon, CR9 3WZ

Offer valid in UK only and is not available to current Reader Service™ subscribers to this series. Overseas and Eire please write for details. We reserve the right to refuse an application and applicants must be aged 18 years or over. Only one application per household. Terms and prices subject to change without notice. Offer expires 31st May 2005. As a result of this application, you may receive offers from Harlequin Mills & Boon and other carefully selected companies. If you would prefer not to share in this opportunity please write to The Data Manager at PO Box 676, Richmond, TW9 1WU.

Mills & Boon® is a registered trademark owned by Harlequin Mills & Boon Limited.
Medical Romance™ is being used as a trademark. The Reader Service™ is being used as a trademark.

WIN a romantic weekend in PARiS

To celebrate Valentine's Day we are offering you the chance to WIN one of 3 romantic weekend breaks to Paris.

Imagine you're in Paris; strolling down the Champs Elysées, pottering through the Latin Quarter or taking an evening cruise down the Seine. Whatever your mood, Paris has something to offer everyone.

For your chance to make this dream a reality simply enter this prize draw by filling in the entry form below:

Name _____

Address _____

_____ Tel no: _____

Closing date for entries is 30th June 2005

Please send your entry to:

Valentine's Day Prize Draw
PO Box 676, Richmond, Surrey, TW9 1WU

Terms and Conditions

1. Draw open to all residents of the UK and Eire aged 18 and over. No purchase necessary. To obtain a copy of the entry form please write to the address above. All requests for entry forms from this address must be received by 31st May 2005. One entry per household only. 2. The offer is for one of three prizes of two nights free accommodation in Paris for two adults sharing a twin or double room and based on flights and accommodation being booked as a package. Flights cannot be booked separately or arranged through any other travel company or agent, and are dependent on availability. Holiday must be taken by 31st December 2005. Restrictions on travel may apply. 3. No alternatives to the prize will be offered. 4. Employees and immediate family members of Harlequin Mills & Boon Ltd are not eligible. 5. To be eligible, all entries must be received by 30th June 2005. 6. No responsibility can be accepted for entries that are lost, delayed or damaged in the post. 7. Proof of postage cannot be accepted as proof of delivery. 8. Winners will be determined in a random and independently supervised draw from all eligible entries received. 9. Prize winner notification will be made by letter no later than 14 days after the deadline for entry. 10. If any prize or prize notification is returned as undeliverable, an alternative winner will be drawn from eligible entries. 11. Names of competition winners are available on request. 12. As a result of this application you may receive offers from Harlequin Mills & Boon Ltd. If you do not wish to share in this opportunity, please write to the data manager at the address shown above. 13. Rules available on request.